Scacciato

a novel by

William S. Maddox

In Memory of Everette Maddox

Cover Illustration by Manfred Pollard

Backcover photo by Tanya Manslank

Published by **Portals Press**
4411 Fontainebleau Drive
New Orleans, Louisiana, USA 70125

Library of Congress Catalogue Number 96-069533

Scacciato

PROLOGUE

Many years ago, a man named Giovanni Boccaccio wrote a book called *The Decameron*. In that book, he told the story of Madonna Beritola and her sons. Madonna Beritola was married to the governor of Sicily, Arighetto Capece, courtier to the bastard Manfred, King of Sicily. When Manfred was killed in battle by the French in 1266, Capece was thrown into prison. His pregnant wife fled the island with her young son Giusfredi and a nurse. A second son, The Outcast (called Scacciato), was born while the family was in flight. While waiting out bad weather on the island of Ponza, the two children and their nurse were taken by pirates and later sold into slavery. Madonna Beritola (later called Cavriuola, The Doe) lived with the wild deer on the island for years, burying her grief in withdrawal from the human race. When she was finally rescued, she became attached to the household of an Italian nobleman, not knowing that Giusfredi had become a servant there. Giusfredi had fallen in love with Spina, the nobleman's daughter, but when they were caught together they were both put in prison. In time, mother and son found each other, Giusfredi was freed, and he married his master's daughter. Later, Giusfredi was able to locate The Outcast and have both him and the nurse freed from slavery. Scacciato's former master gave him his young daughter as a promised bride to make up for his trials. Meanwhile, the Sicilians had rebelled against the French, returning Capece to his post as governor. The family was reunited in a state of wealth and privilege in Sicily. As Bocaccio put it: "There it is believed that they all lived long and happily, at peace with the Almighty and grateful for the blessings He had bestowed upon them." Perhaps. Perhaps not.

I

The Outcast - Scacciato - sat brooding, impatiently watching the evening banquet. His brother and new wife Spina were the guests of honor; both revolted him with their gaiety and empty optimism. His father, the fool, the dupe of politicians, the father he had only recently met, fourteen years after his birth, infuriated him by his very existence. Only his mother Cavriuola appealed to him at all. She still moved like the deer she had lived with for years, in small quick movements fluid and cautious. Although she clearly relished her return from exile, she seemed apart from the celebration somehow and he imagined that, beneath her laughter, she understood his disgust. Merely the second son, not even worthy of a real name, not even raised by her, he believed that he meant something to her, more than the rest of the family did. A tremble of doubt moved through his back and shoulders. He poured himself more wine to drive it away.

He looked again at his mother. Cavriuola - her real name was Madonna Beritola Caracciolo - moved quickly with small bites from one dish to another; the food clearly occupied more of her attention than her family. Apart from Scacciato's promised bride, the little girl d'Oria, hers was the only brown hair at the table among the muzzles and tufts of black. It set her apart from them but not as much as her mannerisms did. Her long face jerked from side to side but froze for a few seconds when she wanted to concentrate on someone's talk or on some taste of food or sometimes on a sound from outside. She held her head, indeed her whole body, more still for those few seconds than ordinary humans can, then returned to the continuous motion that was more natural for her, even though that motion told her younger son that she was no longer quite all there. Scacciato watched her run her hand through her hair which lay light brown down her back and below her waist, exaggerating her thinness. The eyes that moved rapidly from food to family and back to food were dark, almost black. She looked like a tall thin tree with brown leaves and black berries. Except for the movement, the inexorable movement that made her madness, as well as her beauty come alive.

Someone passed a silver bowl of fruit in front of him and it distracted his attention from his mother. He caught a glimpse of his reflection in the bowl. He admired his black hair, his deep-set lively eyes, his large, sharp nose, the strength that showed in his wide lips. But he hated the weakness of his chin; he automatically covered it with his hand and felt for whiskers. He wished every day to look older, to have a face that matched his soul, to have a beard as thick as the growth around his heart.

When he tried to look at his mother again he was filled with anger and confusion. The Nurse was his mother, his father too, had been for virtually all of his fourteen years. She had played the part well, had protected him as best she could, taught him, cared for him, but had never allowed herself to play the part completely, never to touch him, never to reach for him and hold his loneliness next to her, never to say to him "I love you." Now the Nurse sat in some quiet part of the mansion, probably taking a simple meal by herself, protected and secure for her remaining years, but never to be family again.

He stood up and slapped his hands on the table. "I need some air." He said it just as a means of excusing himself but once he had made the proclamation, it became true. The air in the banquet hall was stale, heavy from too many foods with conflicting smells and from too much forced conversation. His parents were involved in talk with Spina, their new daughter-in-law; only his brother Giusfredi noticed that he stood up.

"Return soon," Giusfredi said. "So that we may toast the next wedding."

Scacciato glared at his brother and said "That will be some time." He walked down the length of the wooden table to reach the doorway and passed Guasparrino d'Oria, the man who had been his master for fourteen years, passed out in his chair. As he walked by d'Oria's daughter, Emelia, he realized that the man who had been his master would, in a few years, be his father-in-law. She was only eleven years old and giddy with the excitement that sometimes visits a child when they are the only one in a room full of adults.

"Where you going, Scacciato?"

"Away from here," he snapped.

"Lummox," she said.

He ignored her, hurried through the doorway and then down a narrow corridor used by servants. When he reached the massive kitchen where a half dozen cooks and servers bustled, creating yet more food for the celebrating family, he stopped and thought of his childhood as a kitchen slave. He had spent the days from dawn to midnight peeling vegetables, cleaning fowl and fish, scrubbing pots, hauling refuse out to the back yard, scrubbing pots, delivering food to the table, pouring wine. Then more scrubbing, dragging, cleaning, and pouring until d'Oria's feast was finally over and he could curl up to sleep, exhausted and dirty, on a pantry shelf.

He darted across the back corner of the room to another door and a stairway which led to a wooden porch that ran along the entire length of the house. He stepped heavily along the porch, enjoying the flopping sound he made and the way it echoed across the gardens to the woods and back. He looked up and saw that the sky was odd: in places it was a vast purplish blue with stars visible but most of the sky was filled with clouds of every imaginable shade of darkness, rolling and smashing into each other, rapidly changing shape to form animals, then faces, then mountains, each shape foreboding and cast with a look of permanence even though each one converted itself into something else in less than a minute. He watched for a few minutes with the wind chilling him in his thin shirt and sandals but soon most of the clouds had blown away and he bounded down the wide perron of wooden steps into the garden.

At the foot of the perron was a gravel path which led to a fountain, painted blue and glowing under the stars, about a hundred feet away. Laurel trees dotted the grounds and thick hedges with flower plants at their roots lined the path. The gardens were beginning to repond to the care of the gardeners trying to correct the years of neglect when French officers used the governor's mansion for their home, caring little for the grounds, not knowing how long they would be in Sicily representing the papacy or if their throats would be slit by locals during the night, the Sicilians reputed to be able to tiptoe along gravel paths without turning a single pebble. Scacciato did not know where he was going except that he wanted to follow the path around the mansion, then perhaps walk in the woods or go back inside. He walked loudly, shuffling rocks as a small child whistles walking through darkness. He was only a few feet away from the steps when he heard it.

"Hey asshole."

He slid to a halt and made a full turn but saw nothing in the starlit vegetation.

"What? Who is it? What did you say?"

"I said hey asshole," came the voice, nasal but like sound coming from a vacuum, resonant and high-pitched, almost echoing, coming from some empty space in which sound had only itself to bounce against. The shrubbery beside Scacciato rustled, down low. A human head almost as long as a horse's poked through. In a leap, the rest of the creature was out, although the rest of him did not amount to much.

"Who are you?" Scacciato asked, his voice trembling slightly. He covered his chin with the palm of his hand and rubbed the side of his face with his fingers. "Better yet, what are you?"

"I'm a dwarf, you jerk." He jumped a couple of times to call attention to the truncated legs. When he jumped he barely cleared two inches from the ground. "Duh-warf! Duh-warf! You got it?"

Scacciato got it. His normally recessed eyes bugged to observe the visitor, this troll of the hedge. Light brown hair stuck up all over his head, except on the forehead where the receding hairline made the head look even larger than it was. The skin there was yellowish tan, blotchy, not healthy looking. Below the long forehead, almost in the middle of the hideously swollen squash-shaped head, were eyes that cooled Scacciato's blood, froze his spine so that he could not run away. They were the crazed orange eyes of a pigeon. Many times Scacciato had sneaked out of Guasparrino d'Oria's kitchen to throw crumbs to the pigeons that flew to him at the back step and he had thought: what mad little birds with their eyes of deranged orange and black impenetrable centers. All those times came back to him now as this dwarf with the same lunatic eyes stood below him. Even apart

12

from the eyes, the dwarf was repulsive. A bulbous ocher nose drooped over lips wide and slitheringly thin. The trunk of his body was almost the size of a normal man's but looked smaller underneath his elongated head. Stubby hands with thumbs like large pickles stuck out of his rough tunic. What seemed to be the cut-off pants of a full sized man kept his little legs mercifully hidden. His feet were bound in rags, wrapped bandage-like, the bandages white but stained with mud and grass. Scacciato had heard of dwarfs, had seen a pair of them once on market-day, a finely dressed couple followed by a servant as they bought countless luxuries from the stalls. Perhaps they had been court favorites or rich performers. But he had never seen anything like this yellow apparition from the bushes.

"You're no prize yourself, kid."

Scacciato indeed had been staring in disgust. He shook his head and tried to clear his mind of the confusion that the little man had brought to him. What was this horrific dwarf doing in the bushes of the garden? Briefly his mind wandered back to thoughts of his family, back to the banquet which suddenly seemed less repulsive and unsettling.

"Why are you here? Have you lost your circus?" As he spit out the insult, he took courage from his own voice. This was, after all, only a small intruder. "Be gone. Leave our gardens at once."

"Oh yes, oh yes," the dwarf murmured. He stuck one of his swollen thumbs into his mouth and sucked on it, as if it gave him nourishment. Instead it seemed to remind him of why he was in the garden. "I have come to see you, lad. You see ..." Here he took a long revolting slurp on the thumb. "You're my latest adventure." He smiled insipidly, on either side of the thumb.

"Adventure? What are you talking about?"

"I'm assigned adventures, you see." He spoke in the tedious and methodical whine of a schoolmaster, pedantic and condescending, a whine that threatened to cross over into a squeal at any moment, yet there was a curious bell-like character to the voice as well. "One at a time," he whined and tolled simultaneously. "Never more than one at a time, my adventures."

"What in the hell do you mean by adventures? Am I a game you're playing?" Scacciato was absorbed against his will in the strange

13

creature.

"A game, yes, a game." Slurp. "Precisely that, a game, my little outcast, a game. One game at a time. I am assigned one, you see ..."

"Assigned? Who assigns you?" The dwarf laughed and Scacciato felt chills all over his back and arms. It was the laugh of witchcraft, of demons, of an underworld existing simultaneously with the normal world, a shadow land just around the corner, in dark cracks in familiar places.

"My boy, I haven't the the faintest. Perhaps I am just an adventure for someone else. All I know is that I am called for my abilities, my skill for knowing, for discerning things, seeing the future, that sort of thing." He wiggled a stubby hand to downplay the importance of his psychic skills. "They summon me and say to me - I am called Little Vision - they say to me: Little Vision, here is your next project. I don't really ever see them or hear them, you understand, not exactly. But they say to me: Little Vision, here is your new adventure. Get to work."

"And what is it you do when you get to work?"

"I follow you around. Not physically so much, although I did wait for you tonight. But I follow you around up here ...." He thumbed his broad flat temple. " ... and foresee what's going to happen to you, so I can let you know, sort of, or maybe not let you know, or maybe ... just forget it." He laughed and stared at Scacciato, drilling him with round orange eyes. Little Vision sucked his thumb thoughtfully, then continued.

"I can see everything, you know. Or almost everything, I think. Well, most things. Yes, I can definitely see most things. Some things, at least." He slurped and looked troubled. "Now and then I can see some stuff, but it's not very clear. No, sometimes it's pretty clear although most of the time it's mostly murky, I think. I'm not always sure when it's clear and when it's murky. It's hard for me to tell which is which. Although sometimes I'm absolutely sure of which is clear and which is murky, there are lots of times. No, only now and then, yes," he said with a flourish of his arms. The dwarf looked pleased with himself.

Scacciato felt homicidal. He thought of lifting Little Vision to eye-level but changed his mind. Perhaps he could just walk away and forget this little annoyance. But what if this creature could tell him something about the future? How wonderful it would be to hear someone speak of the future and not of the past! "So you will tell my fortune, is that it?"

"Not exactly that. Well not simply that, at any rate." Little Vision collapsed his legs and sat comfortably crosslegged on the ground. "Have a seat, son," he said, as if in a parlor of his own. Scacciato obeyed, curious and slightly less disturbed now by the dwarf. "What happens is this. This is how it works." He gazed up into the sky, reading it for cues. "It's like this. Um. You see, I'm given an assignment, one assignment at a time."

"All right, we went through that."

"Yes, right, yes. Well, my task is simply to observe and try to discern ..." He glanced again at the sky and stuck a thumb in his mouth. He began to talk with the thumb still there, then realized that only mush was coming out, and started over with an empty mouth. "... try to discern what is going on with you, what it is that is of some importance about you or to you. That is, try to find what important things you should know, if there are any, that is, and ... try to ... um, somehow, um ... communicate these things to you." He smiled, apparently relieved, then he attacked the thumb again, obviously thinking that he would have a moment or two to work on it. Scacciato's quick question annoyed him.

"Why you?"

"Because I can see things, boy. I'm prescient, psychic, I can read dreams and signs and portents, that's why. I can find truth under a rock and read nonsense in a man's face. And I know what is real and what is important, what is not merely tripe." A night chill moved through the starlit gardens. Scacciato shivered slightly; Little Vision shuddered and rubbed his arms.

"And what do you see for me?"

He wiggled his feet in the gravel and smiled. "For you, yes, for you. I see the bist in you."

"The bist? You mean the best?" The young man's eyes sparkled with hope for a fortune-telling full of bright promises.

"No, no, listen to me, boy. The bist, I said. Have you never heard of the bist?"

"Never. What are you talking about?"

"The bist, you see ..." He wiggled again with the joy of a story-teller. "The bist is a small creature, found here in Sicily mostly in pools and streams up in the hills, but found all over the continent wherever it is not too cold and there is fresh water. A lovely little character, well not actually lovely, more on the disgusting side I suppose, but interesting, yes, definitely interesting."

Scacciato glanced around the garden, suddenly wondering if anyone was watching. The blue-painted fountain caught his eye for a moment, reminded him of his father, the past, and the things he wished to think about when the night was over. But this Little Vision intrigued him; perhaps there was something worth hearing in all the sputtering talk from the pigeon-eyed mystic. With a nod, he settled down to listen.

Little Vision went on, periodically giving his thumb a loud suck for nourishment or emphasis or just to annoy his listener. "The bist has a very short life span, only a few weeks. That's why many people do not know about them. They're here and then ..." He fluttered his fat little fingers. "... they're gone. They look a lot like frogs, little palm-of-the-hand sized things, green and brownish with little spindly front legs, a head that just expands to form the body, mostly stomach, then these long bent back legs, no tail. Frogs, just like frogs. Born as tadpoles, in fact. Swim around as tadpoles a couple weeks, then in a matter of a few more days - bam - they're crawling out on land all grown-up and ready to mate. Immediately they start mating, go at it nonstop for a day and a night, then as soon as the sun comes up again, they're done, spent and empty."

"Fascinating."

"Have patience, boy. Now you see the females go right off and make nests on the edge of the water and wait it out. A few weeks later they deliver the babies, the tadpoles, in the water and die on the spot. Yes, momma kicks the old bist bucket right there. Very sad. Not too much to it. But the males - that's another story. A better story, too. A male bist is a creature of appetite, no reflection, least not that you can tell. Of course they may be thinking all kinds of great stuff in there..."

"On with it!" Scacciato recognized a hint of his father's growl in his voice and hated it. "Please," he said, more softly.

"Yes, yes. The male, now, the male bist, what a character, what a peculiar little phenomenon. You see, once his sexual needs are fulfilled, the rest of his life is devoted to ... no, centers around ... no, really is dominated ..." He stopped to suck his thumb while pondering. Scacciato ground his teeth. " ... is ...is ... consumed! His life is consumed with eating! Eating, that's it. Done with procreation and sexual pleasure, he turns to eating. He eats constantly, barely sleeping, exercising only enough to get to the nearest piece of food. He eats bugs, he eats little tiny things that grow on the water, he eats bits of leaves and small sticks, vermin, feces, rot, slime, bilge, dead things, live things, whatever he can get into his big mouth. He becomes an eating thing, a thing that eats, an eater, he no longer is - he eats. And he swells up, of course. That pliable skin stretches and stretches until he's twice or thrice his previous size. But he continues to eat. The bist eats and eats until finally - only a few days, actually - he gets full. He's done again, another need satisfied. Then the weirdest thing happens. He throws up."

"What?"

"He throws up a lot."

"Huh?"

"He never stops throwing up."

"That's weird."

"He'll sit somewhere, usually wherever he stopped eating, and throw up again and again. Over and over. For days he throws up, all day and all night. The poor little thing just goes on and on. Then he's down to normal size, even gets a little emaciated, but he cannot stop, so he begins to throw himself up."

"What?"

"First you notice his little toes on his back feet. They implode, like someone sucked them outside in and then - bleep - there they are in front of him. Then the little feet - bleep - all over the place like a lost lunch. Then his little shins come up and his cute little knee-bones and his little pudgy thighs ..." Little Vision wiped a tear from one round orange eye and sucked the salty thumb. The tears continued but so did he. " ... and his little back end, and his guts, and then his big old tummy. The poor little thing just upchucks himself all over the ground." He fought back the sobs. "Finally his tiny arms go and most of the head until you're left with nothing but this cute little mouth resting on its lips with nothing behind it and then - urp - it kinda turns inside out and pops into the air like from a slingshot. The poor little bist is gone."

Scacciato was horrified, transfixed by the picture of the bist in his mind, mesmerized by the telling of the story. But a moment after the story ended, his tension returned and he blurted out "What's this got to do with me?"

Little Vision smiled through the tears, sniffled, and spoke very softly. "That's for you to figure out."

"Ass!" Scacciato dived on top of the dwarf and, forgetting the distastefulness of touching him, put his hands around the pulpy neck, squeezing the skin that felt rough and broken like tree bark. Little Vision fought to escape; with a lurch he found enough play in Scacciato's grip to move his head to where he could imbed his teeth in his assailant's forearm. For a few seconds, they lay groaning at each other. Then Scacciato had to let go. He doubled over, rubbed the bitten arm, and heard the rustle of shrubbery. When he could raise his head and focus his eyes enough to see through the rivulets of sweat and tears on his face, the dwarf was gone. He stumbled around the garden for a while, cursing and grumbling like a lunatic. When the pain eased and he felt calmer, he ran up the steps, intending to go inside, but changed his mind and stopped at the edge of the porch. He took a deep breath and turned to look toward the gardens. He could see nothing and dropped his head to look down the perron.

On the last step, a pair of lizards fornicated, moving in tiny twitches. As Scacciato watched, he breathed in the coolness of the air as if to store it away to last him through the summer, then looked again at the sky, emptying his thoughts into the heavens, exchanging his uneasiness for the vast calm which men believe exists up there. Then the thought of the fable of the bist returned and, like an anvil tied around his neck, bent his head toward the earth again, aiming his eyes downward to watch the lizards. They had become a tiny green statue, two pieces of a child's puzzle locked and mounted together.

He looked at them impatiently. Why don't they do something? he thought. Did they finish while I wasn't looking? Believing that they were through, he stared dejectedly and wondered if lizards, like humans sometimes, find uncoupling to be an awkward event, a moment in which embarrassment returns achingly after its period of banishment during love-making. Suddenly the tender green statue shuddered and they ran away from each other into diferent parts of the shrubbery. It was only then that Scacciato realized that there had been footsteps behind him. He turned to face his father. He put his sore arm behind him, and leaned against the balustrade.

Arighetto Capece was a large man, coarse and jowly, with a voice that growled in short bursts, the result of rarely speaking during fourteen years in prison. Unlike his sons, he wore his hair long around his neck and matched it with a chest-length black beard turning gray.

"Let me speak with you, son," Capece said. He shuffled forward and stopped only a foot away from his son, then stared at Scacciato to force him to respond.

"Speak," he said, his voice like the tap of a wooden mallet. "Speak all you want."

The old man drew himself up to his full six feet, relaxed his shoulders to form a square barricade, another barrier for the young man. He sighed, then squinted, shifted his weight to the left foot, back to the right, growled slightly.

"What's your problem, boy?"

"Nothing," he said, pausing, "and everything."

"You're getting older, Scacciato. You probably have a stirring in your loins. This is making you uncomfortable." Capece's last sentence was half statement, half question.

"I've had a woman. A slave girl of d'Oria's."

"Then what is making this nonsense in your head?" he asked, losing patience. "What is making you bitter and rancorous? You are the son of a rich and powerful man, Scacciato."

"You don't understand. You don't care about me. You don't care about this family. All you care about is politics."

"I will overlook that because you have suffered much." Arrighetto Capece flapped his big arms, then folded them as he thought of what good news to mention next. "You have a promised bride with a magnificent dowry. Guasparrino d'Oria is an idiot, it is true, a half-wit at best. But as a merchant he is enchanted. He makes money without trying. And her dowry will leave you comfortable for life, free of care and worry, free of politics, not dependent on the fortunes of kings as I have been. You only have to marry her."

"She is eleven years old."

"She will be older."

"So I fear."

"You have a loving mother. And a brother who cares about you."

"My mother thinks she is a deer. My brother thinks he is a man. Both are mistaken."

"What is it you want?" Arrighetto swelled, squinted, and flapped, all at once.

"For starters, a name of my own. I don't want to be The Outcast."

"Call yourself what you want, then! Pick a name! We will no longer call you Scacciato, we will use whatever name you choose."

"A man earns a name. He does not just pick one."

"Nonsense! You're an impossible son! You will make me mad."

"Good. A son should leave his father an inheritance instead of the reverse."

The old man sighed and turned away, looking out over his estate and the woods that surrounded the governor's mansion. In the empty darkness beyond, he could not see the fields that were now his again. He hoped those fields, lying fallow for so long, would make him comfortable again and provide him with the peace and obedience that his younger son refused to give.

"You attach no importance to your inheritance, then?" He did not face his son but stared hopefully into the dark fields.

"I attach great importance to my past, to your past rather. I wish very much to be free of it."

"There is no such freedom," the old man said calmly. "No man walks this earth without the cloak of the past around his shoulders. It is true. Just as there is no Sicily without the Romans and the Moslems and the Normans and the Germans, there is no Scacciato without Arrighetto Capece and there is no Arrighetto Capece without my father and without King Manfred or King Frederick."

"The thought of it is sickening to me." Scacciato had not moved except for his tongue and lips since he braced himself against the balustrade.

Arrighetto seemed not to hear. "The charge we carry is unshakeable, the history undeniably bold and magnificent, no less so now that it is mostly in ruins and buttressed only by the help of ambitious Spaniards. King Frederick united the Normans and the Germans in one body, one soul, one ruler. When his Norman mother gave birth to him under an open public tent to dispel the rumors that she was not with child, too old to bear the new emperor, when she lay wide-open for the eyes of every mongrel peasant who stopped his painted cart long enough to see, she was announcing the beginning of something glorious, a political event comparable to the birth of Christ. In blending her blood with the German ancestry of her husband, she delivered more than a man. In Frederick she presented us with an ideal, a ruler and a scholar and a man of insatiable courage."

"A man whose own doctor tried to poison him as I recall," Scacciato pointed out. "A man who had to fight to hold his own people in check, to keep his harem intact, to battle excommunication by the Pope."

Arrighetto swivelled to face his son, then squinted and turned away again. "They feared his power, hated his courage, envied his openness to the wisdom of all nations, whether Christian or Moslem. The man with the heart to build an empire is always feared. The man with the open mind that grasps and uses the intellect of the whole race is always hated. No wonder he lived in turmoil. No wonder the Pope saw him only as a rival and hounded him all his life into making a doomed crusade. No wonder he would dream up things to ask Frederick to do, knowing that Frederick would refuse and thus create the grounds for excommunication."

"And why should I care about all this?"

"Because it is your heritage, damn you!" Arrighetto Capece reddened and smashed his palm on the railing. "Because it is what came before you and made the world into which you were born!"

He calmed and went on with his story. "He tried to forge a new civilization. Out of the remnants of Rome and the world of the Moslem and the Jew. He tried to open his mind and heart to all that had preceded him here in Sicily and throughout the continent. He was not afraid to accept it all, the burden of the past and the lessons of history." He stopped and sighed. "But they all fought him, the Pope and the small-minded merchants all along the coast, those who can only see their ships as loaded or empty. What is learning, what is history to a merchant?" He spit the word out. "Merchants. Trading in goods or trading in souls, they are all merchants. Is that what you want to be, Scacciato? A merchant for whom the past is nothing?" Scacciato exhaled an excruciating disgusted breath, as if he had held it throughout the conversation and had finally heard something repulsive enough to require letting it out.

"But it was not over when the bug got Frederick, when he shit his guts out and died," the old man continued. "His son Conrad tried to carry on but he was never a strong boy, he died in four years. But Manfred - the bastard king Manfred - he fought on with the anger of the illegitimate son, the fire of bastardy on his side. God, he loved a fight." He spoke now of a man he knew personally, a man he had served as governor of Sicily, had served after his death by rotting in prison, had served by being guilty of allegiance. His voice softened even though the words he used were more harsh. "The bastard king of Sicily, the king who wanted to fight, to slash the throats of the demons who tortured his father's life."

"Is this going to take long?"

"What's wrong with you, boy?" Again he did not turn to look at his son.

"Nothing, go ahead." Perhaps if I let him get through this he will leave me alone, Scacciato thought. Then I can go for a walk to clear my head of this dusty conversation or go to my room and think about this night.

"This is your heritage, Scacciato. Your name - The Outcast - should be a source of pride. Your father governed this beautiful rock, our Sicily, while King Manfred was off defending the name and the dreams of Frederick. Then when Manfred was slaughtered by the French in the name of that devil Pope at Benevento in 1266, I was thrown in prison with the murderers and the thieves and pederasts, and then, only then, were you born outcast, not even knowing who you were, who your father was, or where your mother was, raised in secrecy by your nurse. But now you can carry your name and your family to the greatness, the glory, the recrudescence of the dream of

Frederick, the Kingdom of Sicily, the ..."

"Suppose I told you that all of this is yesterday's ashes to me? I don't care at all about Frederick or the bastard Manfred or you. This legacy you proclaim is a burden to me, an annoyance."

"All right," he said, growling just a little. "All right!" He flapped again. "I know it's been hard for you. Stolen by pirates, sold to d'Oria, working as a kitchen slave all your childhood years, taught to read and write in hiding by your nurse ..." He turned at last to face his son, grasping the railing near him. "But that's over! All of the misery is over! You're free now. You are not a kitchen slave."

"Well, it was a hell of a childhood."

"Ah. So you're jealous because Giusfredi broke away and you did not? He is eight years older than you! You were but a child. Are your feelings hurt because someone else sprang you before you were old enough to do it yourself?"

Capece's words were too close to the truth; Scacciato kept quiet, thinking. And what if it is true, old man? What if I, like anyone with a heart and a brain and any balls at all, wanted to free myself, rather than be freed by strangers. What if I wanted to begin my life with an exertion of will, an act of courage that Arrighetto Capece speaks of so rapturously when it is Frederick, rather than merely his second son, who acts, who fights with the world, who challenges the expected, the usual, the obvious?

"Will you rejoin us?" The old man was calm again, although he breathed heavily.

"I don't know." His arm was beginning to throb where Little Vision had bitten him but he did not want to massage it in front of his father. He wanted to scream at Capece, force him to admit that if he had not been embroiled in politics and the whims of kings and popes they might still be a family and his second son would not be called The Outcast. But it would not come out.

"Very well," Capece said. He looked back and forth from his son to the garden several times, then shook himself a little and walked back inside. Scacciato rubbed his arm and paced across the porch for a few minutes but then was struck with the urge to bring the evening to an end, terminate his part in this celebration of a family reunited, but not yet a family, in his mind.

Instead of retracing his route through the kitchen, he went through the doors from the portico to the second floor, then followed the stairwell down to the ground floor where another corridor separated the banquet rooms. He walked slowly toward the boisterous sounds of eating and talk. When he reached them, he stood half exposed but unnoticed in the doorway.

His father sat on the the right side of the table next to Cavriuola. He kept his arms folded on the table in front of him most of the time; he flapped them in the air occasionally as if bored or uncertain how to behave. When Cavriuola touched his arm, he squinted his eyes and looked off into the distance or gazed at Spina with something in his eyes that Scacciato could not identify. At the near end of the table seated facing each other were his brother Giusfredi and his new wife. Scacciato tried to recall the brother he had known in d'Oria's kitchen and how they had put metal pots on their heads and chased each other around with wooden spoons when no one was nearby. But this man was a stranger. Giusfredi laughed with the frenzied delight of a man whose life had turned from the desperate to the joyful and he frolicked around the table to bring Spina tastes of new dishes as they appeared. His face was the same as Scacciato's only larger and with a dazed and slightly stupid look. As the tall young man sprawled at the head of the table, his giant face rubbery with pleasant confusion, he looked like he was constantly on the verge of making some ridiculous and embarrassing noise.

Scacciato turned to look at Spina. He knew that she had been a young widow when she met Giusfredi and that she was now the center of his world, infusing him with joy and childlike whimsy. Her face was thin but open and accepting, beautiful from the absence of startling features, and framed with black hair. Beneath that face, she was plump, but voluptuous. She spilled and squeezed out of her gown of celebration at every available spot, the skin about to burst through at countless points. Scacciato imagined her taking the heavy spiderous Giusfredi into her arms and breasts and legs and bouncing him joyfully as if she had been created for that one purpose, to give a home to this man's sprawling frame and heart. For some reason he could not articulate, he did not trust her.

Beyond them, on the left side of the table, Guasparrino d'Oria

24

had emerged temporarily from his gluttonous stupor and was laughing at the childish jokes his daughter told him as she wiggled in his lap and played with her waist-length light brown hair. Scacciato remembered that she had cried so shamelessly and violently when the ship was two hours out of port on its way to bring them all home to Sicily that Arighetto Capece ordered the captain to turn the ship around, then went ashore and found d'Oria and offered to take him with them, accept him as a member of the household, even find him something to do under the new regime if he would only come with her and stop the child from crying.

Suddenly, the sight of the two of them content with each other made Scacciato step back and look at the entire group, realizing as he did that they were three couples and that there was no place there for him. I suppose I am still The Outcast, he told himself. He turned and ran back down the corridor, then climbed the stairs as if there were demons on his heels, and quickly entered his second-floor room. With the door bolted behind him, he relaxed and looked at the room, kept simple at his request: a plain bed, a trunk for his things, a small short writing table with a stool.

He took off his clothes, rolled them into a bundle as he had done when he slept on a shelf in a pantry off Guasparrino d'Oria's kitchen, and placed them under the bed. Every night now he stored his roll under the bed and every morning a servant removed it and folded his clothes neatly in his trunk.

Rubbing his aching forearm, Scacciato walked to the trunk and took out a wide bound journal designed for keeping accounts, stolen from the d'Oria counting house. He carried the diary - he called it his treatise because he thought he would one day write great philosophy in it - to the writing desk and spread it before him. He tried to make sense of all he had seen and heard during the evening but his mind raced uselessly from one thing to another and his arm hurt. Finally he gave up and scrawled across a page of the journal: I HATE DWARFS. Later, in bed, he fell asleep dreaming of frogs.

II

Scacciato sat at his writing desk. He had shoved it against the wall underneath the window where he could write and enjoy the bright morning air at the same time. Usually he worked on the treatise at night before going to bed but today he had to write in the morning if he was to write at all; it was his wedding day. He ignored the pressing thoughts about his first night of marriage, looked at the trees outside his window, and opened the journal. The volumes of his treatise, all old account ledgers like the first he had stolen from Guasparrino d'Oria, filled a locked trunk which sat on the floor, beside the one for his clothes and other belongings. Otherwise, in the seven years since the dwarf had disappeared into the shrubbery, the room had changed in only one respect. While the bed, the trunk, the writing table, and stool were still the only items of furniture, the rest of the floor space was buried under stacks of bound volumes and papers, the fruits and waste of seven years of study, what was left from a succession of tutors brought in at Scacciato's request by his father. They had come bearing hand-copied books, languages, and religious doctrines. Scacciato devoured them, left their bones outside in the hall, and kept the books. The room, once bare and bright, was now dusky and dense with the litter of learning. Tonight he would move his trunk of clothes into the suite of rooms on the third floor that he would share with young Emelia and use this room only for his study.

Scacciato was calmer now than he had been as a child. He still wanted to be free of the past, his father's past, but he had learned patience, embraced the notion of waiting for the proper time. Acts and decision and movements must take place at their right time, not before, a time ordained not by some Creator or master plan or some placement in an everlasting chain of reincarnation and reoccurrence,

26

but by the development of the motives of the actors, the participants.

There would be a time when he would break away, when the fact of his presence on earth would become the major phenomenon of his life and a critical one in the lives of others, but that time was not yet. Thus, he had spent the past seven years as a bit player in the Capece household, a secondary character in his own life, burying himself in trying to learn everything that was available to him, making his presence known only periodically when he had to request a new tutor (the last one drained, emptied, bled of all he could offer) or request some more volumes to be ordered or ask for more journals in which he could write. He lived a shadow life, as an appendage to learning, soaring only in his walks of fantasy in the woods and in reflection late at night when he worked on the treatise.

The treatise: he clung to the grandiloquent name he gave to his work, that which others would have called a journal or even a diary. Each night he wrote his thoughts, feelings, questions. Sometimes he discussed on paper what he had learned or read during the day. Other times he described the day's events in a few words. This, he quickly discovered, disciplined his thought and his communication style, so that he found himself increasingly able to express more in fewer words, thus relieving himself of much tedious conversation but exchanging that tedium for a gnawing impatience with the rambling dialogue of most humans.

As for his family, Scacciato spent little time with them. His father, busy with the task of solidifying his return to power, was rarely at home. Peter of Aragon had reclaimed the throne at the request of the locals in 1282. Thus, Arrighetto Capece spent most of his time in town trying to fit himself into the new regime. When he was at home for a rare dinner with the family, he spent the whole evening complaining about Peter and his nosy wife Constance and the ambiguity of being governor of Sicily when Sicily also had a king.

But Peter died all of a sudden in 1285, dropping off the face of the earth without warning. Constance, daughter of the bastard king Manfred and therefore a local sentimental favorite despite her querulous meddling in politics, could no longer surreptitiously rule the island or extend her long sticky fingers into every crevice of its internal affairs. For three years she had been, in effect, the ruler of Sicily.

Peter played at being king, Arrighetto Capece signed documents and twitched. Suddenly she was just another dowager assigned to a town house, left with nothing to do. There she wasted away in boredom. Perhaps she died, but no one noticed.

Peter and Constance's son James came from Barcelona to rule as Sicily's new king. His first act of power was to banish his mother from the king's estate, put her in town to pasture so to speak and it gave Capece and the locals hope that James would be the kind of king they wanted: strong, outrageous, pugnacious, like Manfred or Frederick. James' energy extended only to his dislike for his mother, however. He promptly lost interest in affairs of state, took to hunting and drinking, and left the daily business of governing to others.

At first disappointed in this latest failure in the line of Frederick, Arrighetto Capece soon realized that he and his Sicilian cronies had been presented with a perfect situation: they had a king who protected them and gave them legitimacy but otherwise left them alone to pursue their own ends in amassing wealth and extending Sicilian influence throughout southern Italy. Capece was rarely at home again.

The rest of the household simply lived and Scacciato had little to do with them. The most active of the family were Giusfredi and Spina. They made babies, about one a year. There were times when Scacciato could take an afternoon away from his studies and enjoy spending some peaceful time with a niece or nephew but most of the time he ignored them. After the first three or four he could not even keep up with their names; it was like trying to name the bushes in the garden or rocks in the path. All he could remember with any certainty was that there was at least one Manfred and one Frederick in the pile. Spina, then, was busy and content, never saying much (clearly never saying no to Giusfredi), taking responsibility for raising the children with very little help from servants. He watched her from his room when they walked in the garden and at meals when the small creatures orbited her and clutched at food. They were the moons and she was the planet, always in quiet efficient motion, never flustered, somehow containing and enjoying three, then four, then five, then six and so on little whirlwinds of eating, shitting, and screaming.

Giusfredi was around the house less often. He had wanted to be a part of his father's clique but his talents for subtlety, diplomacy, and avarice were minimal. They stuck him away to work in a small city twenty miles from the mansion, as chairman of the local council. Capece had established the councils, one roughly every twenty miles, as a way to keep the locals feeling that their island had some democratic elements and to keep the mundane business of settling disputes out of his hair. Each area council of from five to ten men was like a court, hearing arguments in every kind of conflict from business disputes to murder cases, but the council was also the rulemaker and enforcer of laws for the area.

Capece, of course, appointed the chairman of every council. Giusfredi spent his days listening to peasants arguing about who owned such and such goat or pasture. He daydreamed a lot at work, then went home late at night and played with his brood of daydreams and, very late at night, fathered more.

Scacciato tried to get close to his mother for a while but she was no more at home than her husband, even though she never left the mansion. He set aside an hour every morning to visit in her room, to try to catch up on what he had missed, to find out more about her. She sat respectfully in a chair and smiled, nodded, answered his questions simply, patiently, quickly. Finally she told him "You will know me better if we do not speak."

He was not hurt, in fact was encouraged by the thought that he had found a channel through which he could reach her, a new approach to her. He stopped the daily visits and concentrated on meal times when he would watch her, observe every tiny movement, every subtle twitch in her face, thinking that each jerk of the head or fluttering of the eyes or glance over her shoulder was not madness but her way of loving, her means of communication, her unique attempt to create the bond of mother-son love that he wanted and believed that she wanted.

He began to imitate her movements, reflecting and mimicking them back to her, then tried dreaming up his own language of motion just as two creatures from different planets would make sounds and gestures to each other, hoping that they could randomly stumble across that first connection, that one linkage between them, a foundation upon which they could build. He still did not know if he was making any progress the night his father, during one of his rare appearances

29

at the family dinner table, grunted something about twitching imbeciles, did not know as the blushing flag of defeat and aloneness unfurled around his face and neck if he was any closer to Cavriuola than he was when he started. He decided that a man can never know his mother until he is older and gave up for a few years.

Then he had turned to his real mother, the Nurse, but she would not open up to him. He could never get her to explain her background, why she had become his nurse and tutor and cook, his general servant (she had been theirs, Giusfredi's and his, until Giusfredi escaped slavery, then she had become his alone), or even how she happened to know how to read and write, how she knew some Greek and Latin. He always romanticized that she was the child of a famous family gone to ruin and had taken refuge from the unfair world by serving a still prosperous house, only to be thrown into exile and slavery, rescued later in life and returned to a position of comfort. He believed this fantasy about her but she would not confirm it, responding to his questions with a smile and the words "Past is past, Scacciato," unwittingly providing him with a motto of sorts, a point of view he desperately wanted to be his own.

After the return to Sicily, they gave her a little room on the unoccupied third floor of the mansion and let her be to enjoy her old age. She was assigned duties, of course, as was proper: she had to keep the third floor pleasant for when visitors came. But months passed between visitors. Most of the time she simply puttered through the day, enjoyed Scacciato's visits and his rambling discussions of what he was learning (sometimes she could still correct his language or his confused interpretation of some religious passage), and pursued a touching little love affair with Anglico, one of the new gardeners.

Anglico was short and thin and gray (like her), gentle and stupid, but apparently just what the old nurse wanted in a man. It was assumed they would marry someday, the two old love-birds, but no one rushed them and no one complained when the old gardener inched his way up the back stairs to her room at nightfall just as chickens flutter into low-lying tree branches as the sun goes down.

Thus Scacciato had tried his family and found no friendship. Tolerance, even kindness, but no friendhsip. The Nurse was still the closest to either friend or family that he had but she was getting old, inactive, and preoccupied. As many men do with their parents, he had drawn on her for years, received more than he or any child could give. He felt guilty for having drained her and for having as yet little to return. Should not the child take all the parent has to give and then repay it, he wondered? Refill the emptied soul with something? Not a material repayment or simply time spent awkwardly spending time, but something of value to the parent's mind and being? Or is it that, by a certain age, the parent is too drained, too tired to receive, simply wants to be left alone to experience all the things missed before, the pleasures swept aside in the business of living?

Now the Nurse only wanted her comfortable clean rooms and her little old gardener Anglico. She wanted something of Scacciato too, but whether he spoke of gods and nature and man's folly or sputtered about the crops and Spina's contumacious brats tearing up the mansion did not matter. He could simply make noise for all she cared and he knew it. The cold recognition of this drove him more than ever to his studies. There was nothing else in the household for him.

He sat forward and thought: Wait. There is one more element in the family picture. Emelia will become my wife today. Scacciato relaxed at his writing desk to think about her. He stretched his legs under the desk and spread his arms out across the surface, resting in the splayed posture of an insect.

He had grown in seven years, of course. He would now make two of the dwarf Little Vision but Giusfredi, at over six feet, was still at least a head taller. Without much effort or attention, his muscles and bones had become those of a grown man, although there was still a gangliness about him which made him appear larger than he was but also younger than he was. He wore his hair more in the style of his father than he had as a child, long down his neck and over his ears; it softened the sharpness of his face but added even more melancholy to the dark eyes that lingered, unwilling to come out, far back in his head. But the weak chin was gone, at least hidden by a short black beard that covered his lower face tightly like a mask. He assiduously trimmed it every few days to make sure that he did not begin to resemble Arrighetto Capece's beard and his chest-length protrusion of matted hair. As he thought about the d'Orias, however, he covered his chin with his hand, rubbing against his palm the beard that obviated but did not eliminate this nervous gesture left from adolescence.

He thought of Emelia more fondly than usual this day but even that was something of an obligation: a man is supposed to think well of his future wife on the morning of his wedding day. He had watched her grow in passing, without a lot of interest, watching her as he watched the fields, the crops, and the trees around the mansion repeating an annual cycle but at the same time changing each year, the yearly growth and annual repetition. The elders of the household had taught her some, gave her a few years of training, although from local tutors, no one as challenging or as brilliant as the ones they summoned for Scacciato. But she could read and write and knew a few things, advantages that most women, well-born or peasant, did not have. For most women, life was child-bearing and work, whether the work was sweating over the crops alongside a peasant husband or straining to be the proper wife for a nobleman. Either way, they were extensions of men, half-people, creatures who bore children.

Cavriuola had taken an interest in Emelia, and Scacciato took that as another sign of Cavriuola's special attachment to him. She found teachers of music and painting to develop Emelia into an artist of sorts. She grew out of some of her childish giggling and fondling with her father but not all of it. Now a young woman of eighteen, schooled and talented, she still broke into paroxysms of private laughter now and then, at jokes or amusements which no one else heard or saw. Some thought of her as silly for this - Scacciato often did - but the truth was that usually she laughed because she was happy, as some people relax into a deep lasting smile when they think of the goodness or contentment in their life.

d'Oria's daughter did not simply smile: Emelia howled and sometimes screeched with laughter. Since she was happy now, feeling at home in Sicily at last, resigned to and even curious about her arranged marriage, content with her accomplishments in learning and the arts, she laughed a lot.

Her father, resigned to an insignificant government sinecure, had little to do with Scacciato's life. His wealth secure, his home now defined as the Capece household, d'Oria spent most of his time sitting in the taverns telling stories, coming home at night smelling of drink and talking too much, then listening to his little girl sing to him or going for walks with her, observing how she had grown and what she had learned. He was proud of her. She was a woman of leisure, soon to be married to a young man of family and power.

d'Oria was especially pleased with how she had come to look like her mother, his young wife who had died giving birth to Emelia. Since his wife did not live to grow old with him, it seemed to him that she had simply been replaced by the infant who then emerged in eighteen year's time as the same young woman, as if he and the two women experienced some weird process of stuttering evolution. Emelia was attractive but not striking, a beautiful girl who had not become a beautiful woman, too frail, too wispy, not quite even grown or filled out, with hair still too thin to be more than pretty. Her eyes which, in their clearness, had been too old for the child seemed too infant-like for the adult. Guasparrino d'Oria, however, never tired of looking at her.

Scacciato liked the fact that he was taking d'Oria's daughter. He sat back in a chair and smiled.

The past few years had been fairly happy for him. Apart from the loneliness, his life had been pleasant, disciplined, productive, and yet not hard. As he looked back over the years, he remembered a recurring dream in which he saw small animals wretching over and over. Startled by this thought, he threw himself to his feet, retrieved several of the old volumes of the treatise from the trunk, and began flipping through them, looking for something he had written years ago in response to Little Vision's visit. He found the proper volume but paged back and forth for several minutes trying to locate a passage that stuck in his mind. When he found it, he sat the book up on its edges where he could read it with the morning sun of his wedding day as a backdrop.

He read on, fascinated by his own writing. "I live in dreams, in images, in thoughts. My usual response to reality is: what has this got to do with anything? But the dwarf and the bist and the dreams, they are real. Perhaps I made them up and that is why they are real to me. They are the first things that happened to me that I created."

He reread the passage several times, wondering why it had come back to him, called for him, on this morning. A crashing fist on his door broke the spell. It had to be either his father or his brother.

Arrighetto Capece knocked that way because he liked to intimidate people with his bear-like strength and his ability to make noise. Giusfredi knocked that way because he could not help it. Anything he did became loud, crashing, awkward, boisterous, too much, and eventually moronic and unneccessary. If he only stood outside a door without knocking, he could not stand there for more than a minute without bumping into it, leaning loudly against it, or otherwise making some noise which would give away his presence.

Scacciato sighed. It must be my brother out there. He couldn't sneak up on a dead man.

"Come in if you must." He slapped the journal shut, partly to hide his private treatise and partly to startle his mind back into the present, to file away for a few minutes the inexplicable sense of connection he felt between the words written in response to the dwarf's visit and the picture of his bride he had drawn in his mind over the past seven years.

Giusfredi exploded into the room. In a fit of merriment, he had chosen to dress himself in bright colors for the day. He wore a floor-length robe of yellowish-orange with light colored skin boots projecting from underneath. His hat, a ridiculous widebrimmed tan, was topped by an orange plume. He looked like a bedraggled prize at a fair. Although he knew his brother felt cool toward him, he always began his infrequent conversations with Scacciato as if they were the best of friends.

"Ah, my little brother!" In three steps he crossed the room, then grabbed Scacciato by the shoulders. "My little Scacciato gets married today! How do you feel? Are you excited?"

Scacciato rested his back against the desk and smiled. He found his brother amusing for a change, at least partly because of his outlandish outfit. "I am. I am excited. Thank you for your interest."

"Interest? Of course!" He looked a little puzzled. "It will be a wonderful day for us all. A nice big wedding and then lots to eat and drink and then ... ah... " He squeezed his brother's knee. "Going to whack your little bride tonight, huh?" His laughter bellowed off the walls. Scacciato blushed, embarrassed not by the mention of intercourse but only by his brother's simple joy. He lowered his head and shook it back and forth, smiling. Giusfredi misinterpreted the message.

"You do know ...? You know, I mean, you know about what to do ... I mean tonight, you know how ...?"

"Yes, brother, I know all of that."

"Phew. Thank God. You must have ..." He rolled his eyes and wiggled one hand. " ... one of the local girls, maybe one of the maids in d'Oria's kitchen, eh? Long time ago?"

"The Nurse," he lied. Sometimes in conversations that bored him, Scacciato lied, blatantly, sometimes obviously, knowing that if he lied and was caught, it would be amusing and that if he was not caught, it would be amusing in a different way.

"The Nurse?" Giusfredi drew his arms into his sides, aghast and a little impressed. "When? When did you do this?" His voice took on the tone he used when questioning peasants about murder and theft at meetings of the council.

"When I was seven," he lied again.

"When you were seven? Could you ... you know ... could you ... when you were seven? Ah, you little asshole! You joke your brother!"

He grabbed the shoulders again and shook Scacciato, who could not help giving in to share his brother's laughter. "She is a very pretty woman, your Emelia," he began again .

"Yes, she is," Scacciato said.

He hoped she would be as smart as she was pretty. She had some talent for music and painting and that was a good sign. He worried that he knew so little about her but realized that he probably knew his betrothed better than most young men in his position would know the women they were promised. It struck him suddenly that he had long ago accepted the arrangement, the marriage that was the continuation of the past he had hated most when he first came to Sicily. He accepted it even as he despised the rest of the world of his father, the world of the past, the life he tolerated only to use it, to take advantage of the wealth and freedom to learn all he could in preparation for the beginning of his life, whenever that might come. Why? Why had he accepted this marriage? Should he rebel now while he still had a chance?

His brother continued to talk but Scacciato was not listening. He was thinking with eyes glazed over and slightly more recessed than usual, the look that told anyone sensitive enough to notice - Giusfredi talked on - that the brain behind those crystallized eyes was busy elsewhere. Had he made a friend unwittingly, not even desiring it, not speaking of it even to her? Had this accomplice in surrender, surrender to the past and tradition, become his friend and thereby made the surrender less important than the grander struggle he believed he would someday make? Did it make the loss of this one battle merely a propitious phase in the larger fight, the war of the son against the father, the war of youth against age, the fight for uniqueness that every child must endure even though most give up without knowing it, whimper and relax one night in their childhood bed and decide without consciously deciding that they will fight no more?

With that thought, Scacciato's cold and scholarly heart became filled for an instant with joy and a bright yellow warmth like the leaping of flames in a fireplace. He quite forgot that Giusfredi was in the room; indeed, he forgot for a moment to breathe, that is, to exhale. When, involuntarily, he let the air out with a whoosh, blackness devoured him, throwing dank heavy water on the yellow flames, and he leveled at himself the most despicable imprecation he could think of: I know nothing. Quickly the words and the bitterness raced through his mind: I know nothing. I am not yet a man. I am not yet free of the tentacles of my father or the weight of the stones that make my father's house. How can I claim a wife when I am yet a child, still lacking courage and lacking even a name of my own, still The Outcast?

Giusfredi touched his brother's leg. "Are you all right? Are you there?"

"Yes. I"m sorry." He shook his head, trying to dispel the image that was forming before his eyes: a dwarf standing where Giusfredi stood, a dwarf surrounded by little frog-like creatures throwing up. It took him several moments to clear the picture from his mind so that his field of vision was filled with Giusfredi again and the floor no longer felt damp and putrid beneath his bare feet. He returned to the conversation, in control again, although he continued to wiggle his toes squeamishly for a few minutes. "And how are you my brother?" he asked.

"I'm fine," Giusfredi answered, with a confused look on his face. It was clear that he had been in the middle of some topic and had stopped only to find out if Scacciato was still on the planet. Now Giusfredi did not know if he should continue or back up and start over or forget it. Scacciato's attempt at family chatter took him off the hook.

"I don't see you much now with your work and the family, of course. It was a long time ago that we chased each other around d'Oria's kitchen banging pots on our heads and pretending we were monsters."

Giusfredi laughed and slouched, touched by the recollection of that childhood scene. They had always been a little too different in age or in point of view or in what was going on in their lives to be close, but they had shared a few years after Scacciato was old enough to work full time in the kitchen and before Giusfredi ran away from slavery, a few years when both were children in their hearts, before Giusfredi's adolescent restlessness forced him out into the world in an impetuous and aimless blast and before Scacciato knew enough about the world to learn bitterness or to acquire his inchoate and as yet unfocused seriousness.

They shared silently a picture of the past, the two of them chasing each other with wooden spoons, each trying to be the first to ring the other's ears by banging on his iron pot, the iron cookpots they wore like hats when no one was watching during the lazy afternoon break between the midday meal and the preparations for supper. Then Giusfredi started and returned to his earlier line of conversation, the one that Scacciato did not hear.

"So what will you do now?" he asked.

"I don't know." He said it as a proclamation, more than a response to a simple question, as if it was the logical and natural extension of the earlier thoughts that had distracted him from Giusfredi's rambling. He believed that all of his studying, his patience, and the formless anger he had known for seven years was aimed toward something but he did not know what. Somehow he thought that he should know what on this day more than on any of the days that had come before. He felt both amazed and perplexed that he was content to follow the custom of his father's world and marry his assigned woman. He was no closer to knowing what he would do with his life or in what way it would be his life and not his father's and this gave the conversation with his brother an ongoing eeriness.

"You have worked hard, Scacciato. You can be proud. I am proud. I never knew my little pot-scrubbing brother would be a scholar." He smiled and his face expanded, big wooden-looking teeth appearing everywhere, so that the corners of the smile were even with his ears. "But I have wondered - we have all wondered - what you plan to do with all of this." It was not clear if he meant the learning or the piles of paper all over the room. "There is much you could do to help our father. I have tried but I am..."

Stupid, Scacciato thought.

" ... not a politician. You, though, you are smooth. You can size things up with your mind, you keep to yourself until you have it all figured out, you could be of great help to him, to Sicily, to the King."

Moron, he thought. How can he be so blind to the corrupt political life our father has led. But he could not say this to his only brother who was offering friendship on this important day, trying to be closer than anyone had been in years.

"No, I don't want to be a politician. I have no interest in herding peasants or playing court games." He did not consider when he said it that Giusfredi herded peasants all day and would have been happy to be skilled enough to play court games, but his brother did not take offense.

"Hmm. Well, with all your learning ..." He pondered for a moment, as if oppressed by the thought of Scacciato's learning. "You could be, of course ... but you don't want to be a clergyman, do you? You know how father feels about the devilish Pope. It would kill him if you became a priest." For the first and last time, only for an instant, Scacciato felt attracted to the priesthood. "Maybe to be a man of learning, a teacher, a monk or something, but not to join the Papal forces when they have fought to make Sicily an outpost of the Vatican."

"No, no, brother."

Indeed, to fight with the forces against his father was an attractive idea. But he was no more interested in serving the Pope than he was interested in serving Arrighetto Capece or King James of Aragon. He wondered for a moment if it was possible, how it might be possible, to live one's life without serving anyone. He filed the question away for later exploration in the treatise. "No, that is not my kind of life." He paused, trying to think of some way to continue. "Right now, I just cannot think of anything I want to do. Least of all go into the church. Besides, I don't even believe in God."

Giusfredi was shocked but saddened even more. He was deeply and stupidly religious even though he shared - or emulated - his father's distaste for the church hierarchy and its interference in secular affairs. Politics aside, he believed in God, had become even more convinced of God's existence with the birth of each child and here his only brother, living under the same roof, was a nonbeliever.

"I'm ... Im sorry to hear that. Are you sure?"

"If there was a God, I would despise him." He spoke forcefully, unmindful of the effect on his brother. "If there is a God, he is a twisted creature to let most men live the lives of slugs. Those few wealthy and powerful enough to escape that live in dream worlds of pointless self-congratulation. All in all, God is an excuse for avoiding life, a way of wasting life. I would rather risk burning in hell for an eternity than risk wasting this life, the only one I know I have."

He could have said "Giusfredi, your children are all field mice" and the message would have been no less devastating. It was because Giusfredi could not believe that this tirade came from his brother's lips that he was not angry, only confused.

"Well, how we got into this, I don't know," he mumbled. He walked around in a small circle, pretending that he had not really heard. He walked and paused alternately for several minutes while Scacciato awkwardly picked at his fingernails, wondering if honesty was worth the trouble. When Giusfredi spoke again, it was as if he had forgotten the whole thing, at least the part about God.

"Well, if you ... well what else could you do with your life? Have you thought about it? Of course you have. Ah, then, there is your bride's father, right? Oh how I have heard him rave about his managers on the continent, how they steal the third part of everything his business makes him. There you are. He would certainly rather have that third go to you as his new son and manager. How about that?"

Scacciato leaned forward with his elbows on his knees and shook his head. "I have no need of the fortune I could make there. Even if none of this is ever mine ..." He gestured to mean the mansion and estate, paused a second and wondered what he would do with the estate if it ever did become his. "... d'Oria brings me a huge dowry. I do not have to do anything for the rest of my life. Why should I count coins and barrels for that old idiot?"

"Well, you have a point." Giusfredi was more and more uncomfortable with the whole conversation. Perhaps, he thought, this is why I never talk to my brother. Noise from the rest of the house had been increasing gradually; the silence that descended between the two brothers made it seem louder now and gave Giusfredi an excuse to change the subject. "But you have time to think about that. The house is alive with preparations for the wedding. You probably have much to do yourself. I will leave you to your duties. By the way, do you like my choice of clothes for the ceremony?"

"It's lovely." Scacciato smiled and clinched his teeth tightly to prevent himself from laughing out loud.

"Not too bright?"

"Not too bright," he said, thinking of both the outfit and the man inside. He knew that his brother had had enough and was ready to end the conversation but suddenly Scacciato felt compelled to express his concerns to someone - Giusfredi was there - before the day's events proceeded. Even though he knew this man had no answer, might not even understand the question, he stood up and blurted it out anyway, as a man lost in a forest would wrap his fingers around the nearest tree trunk and beg the tree to confess where the exit was hidden. "Shouldn't a man understand something before he gets married? Shouldn't you know what you are going to be, what your life will mean, before you attach yourself to someone else? Shouldn't you be sure of something first?"

"No. I don't think so." The reply was lame, but honest.

They stood awkwardly for a moment, each with a beseeching look on his face: Scacciato making one last attempt to glean something of importance, of some use from his brother's experience and Giusfredi begging his brother to stop. "Enough," Scacciato said. "Enough of this. Go on, my brother." He slapped him on the thick shoulder that he could reach. "Go to your preparations and I will go to mine. Let us have a day of pleasantness together."

"Right! Yes! We will!" Giusfredi's relief spread throughout his face and his long body. He ambled toward the door spewing more congratulations and pleasantries, then all but leaped through the door with laughter and grunts of happiness.

Scacciato sank on to the stool, alone again at last. The sound of his own words sickened him; he rubbed his midsection with one hand and his nose with the other. He stopped for a moment and held his nose, rubbed it all over, felt its contours, thinking how this broad appendage bound him ineluctably to the man who had just left the room. Something in the room was now very oppressive, perhaps the air itself. He could not distinguish between the sourness in his stomach and the putrescent falseness lingering in the room.

The early summer morning air outside promised some relief but as he stood to retrieve his boots, his stomach catapulted to his throat. He leaned one arm on the desk, stiffened, and continued. He had to get out, go for a walk in the woods and sunshine, leave the stench of confusion that clung to him in this room, somehow get through and beyond the cackle and fidgeting of the family, all at home today, all ebullient with their own personal interpretations of what this day meant. He kept on his brown tunic, one like a hunter would wear to camouflage himself in the forest, then stuffed his feet angrily into long boots, and walked to the door before he realized that he had forgotten his pants, realized that the entire interview with Giusfredi would have looked ridiculous to an outsider: a young man with no pants begging for answers to philosophical questions from a giant in yellow and orange. He began to laugh but stopped when the nausea returned. After pulling on the rough trousers that matched the hunting shirt, he leaned against the inside of the door, listened to the family out in the hall, finally took several deep breaths to pacify the rolling demands of his stomach, and stepped out.

When he opened the door, Scacciato peered out at a mansion over two centuries old, a spare and sturdy leftover from the days of the Moslems. There was little to notice about the interior of the place; it may have been a barracks of sorts for early invaders for it included only large square rooms and hallways, converted into specific uses by the custom and habit of several generations of Sicilian rulers. Each floor could contain a small village within its thick walls. The ground floor included grand halls for meetings and parties and ceremonies like today's wedding, two banquet rooms, the expansive rectangular kitchen, and a corridor of rooms for servants. The top floor, where the Nurse reigned as both queen and servant girl, was carved into small chambers, most of them closed off and unfurnished, kept in waiting for the guests who never came because Arrighetto Capece did most of his entertaining in town and even slept there himself most nights and because the rest of the family, each in his own way, lived without need of company.

The second floor, the one Scacciato saw after he forced himself through the door, was divided into suites of rooms for the family: his parents' rooms at the far end facing the gardens, the d'Orias in a small wing which protruded north toward the road that led to town, then an empty set of rooms next to the largest suite (almost a third of the floor) where Giusfredi and Spina played shepherds with their flock, then another collection of empty rooms which served as a buffer between the rest of the house and Scacciato's single chamber on the opposite end of the floor from his parents.

The mansion was in fact a village today, raucous with family activity, rattling from the servant's efforts to get the household in order. Scacciato's wedding clothes lay ready, spread across the bed, but, except for Giusfredi in his screaming orange and yellow, the rest of the family seemed to be in agony over the choice of what to wear. That collective indecision explained why, when Scacciato looked down the long corridor, he saw an agitated Arrighetto Capece talking to Cavriuola, who stood naked in the middle of the hall, oblivious to the frenzy of servants rushing around her carrying dresses and cloaks, apparently unable to find even one garment which interested her. Scacciato made his way slowly down the hall, curious about this scene of confusion despite his urgent need to be alone, his desire to race out into the woods where there was no family, no servants, no wedding.

"You must choose something, woman!" the old man shouted.

"I will, dear," she breathed. "I will in time."

"You could at least put on some clothes!"

"I will wear nothing but the best today. It is my son's wedding. I will only wear something beautiful."

"Can't you go back into your room at least?"

"It is hot in there." She flitted her head back and forth peevishly. Her hands were clasped together in front of her belly; her stillness and posture were those of a statue in a garden.

Scacciato had never seen his mother unclothed before; she was exquisitely beautiful. As he walked slowly toward the couple, he could not take his eyes from her, all of her. He was not shocked or dismayed or even annoyed as Arrighetto Capece was. He was mesmerized by the delightful sight. He had long thought of her as The Doe. Like a fawn caught unaware in the woods or like a cat arrogantly but delicately posed on a stone wall, she presented a posture erect but at ease, a stillness that seemed more alive than the movements of most humans. More than anything else, she seemed correct and proper, peacefully sane amidst the scurrying ridiculous creatures in their swishing cumbersome clothes, the lower life forms trying to force their backward habits on her. Scacciato forgot for a moment that his mother was stark mad.

"Here's your son. Can't you throw on a robe or something?"

"Scacciato," she said, moving only her head. His name had never sounded so mellifluous or so much like a real name.

"Mother," was all he could say.

"I am trying to get your mother ready for this afternoon," Capece grunted. He laughed roughly and flapped his arms. "As you can see, I am not having much luck."

"How are you on your wedding day?" Cavriuolla asked.

"I'm all right." he said, looking only at her eyes.

"Please, Madame Beritola," Capece said.

Fool, he thought. Only you would call her by her full name in anger on this very day when she never looked more like Cavriuola, The Doe, and never looked more content to be Cavriuola.

"Very well, dear," she said wearily. She was not insane enough to fight him. "Until later, my son." She turned and in small silent steps returned to her room.

"Wedding day madness, son," Capece muttered. "I don't know what ..."

"I'm going for a walk," he said, to cut him off. "I'll be back by noon."

He turned and strode down the hall, trying not to think of the old man's staring eyes even though he could feel them sizzling on the back of his neck. He raced to the stairway and then down the steps to the first floor, holding his breath all the way as if there was no air left in the mansion or at least no air that was unpoisoned. Only outdoors, maybe in the woods surrounding the house, could he take a chance and breathe. He hurried toward one of the side doors at the end of a hallway that separated the two long banquet rooms. His search for solitude was doomed, however; there was another obstacle.

Guasparrino d'Oria stood in one of the banquet room doorways, poised where he could reach out and stop Scacciato's escape. Already the old merchant was disgustingly drunk; he did not look as if he would still be awake for the ceremony. His clothes, an old jacket of undefinable color and loose pants of muddy green left from the previous night, hung from his fat like growths. They were rank and wet, smelling of vomit and drink. He was a short corpulent man with a face of pliable pudge, one that looked temporary, arranged in its current configuration only because that is how d'Oria had slept in it the night before. The dark brown eyes like pellets roamed around inside the face. Scacciato always believed that if he slapped the man's head the eyes would rattle.

d'Oria's deplorable state had little to do with the wedding of his only child. Capece had given him a sinecure with the nearest city council and d'Oria's primary duty was to stay away from the council. With his business in Genoa no longer of any interest to him (yes, he complained, often and boisterously that his managers were robbing him but that was only to have something to talk about) and his position in the family and the local power structure both secure and meaningless, the old man drank all day to pass the time. Long excursions to the taverns, embarrassing explosions of gluttony at the family dinner table, occasional walks and visits with Emelia, these habits constituted a life for him. Scacciato loathed the man so much that it was almost intoxicating. While he hated his own father in a way that was cold and rational, he hated d'Oria like a man hates a slug on his pants leg or a cockroach in his soup, violently and viscerally. Scacciato hated Capece in his mind and in his heart; he hated d'Oria in his stomach.

The crapulous father of the bride held the doorway with one arm and wrapped the other around Scacciato to prevent his passing.

"My son!" he said. "My new son today!"

Scacciato released the breath he had been holding. What now? he asked himself. Should I try to be civil to this human rat so as to keep my wedding day as peaceful as possible or should I heave his besotted carcass across the banquet table? He is the last one for me to escape. I've endured the others, let me get through this quickly and then I can be alone to think, to think about my wedding and my bride and my future.

"Hello, d'Oria." He amazed himself with his cheerfulness. "Are you happy or sad today? Are you glad for your child and the beginning of her new life or are you feeling lonely about losing your daughter?" He thought that enough questions would keep the tiny part of d'Oria's brain that was still working occupied, thereby bringing the meeting to a quick end.

"Come drink with me, my new son! No one else in this scrofulous household will. They treat me like a slave. Ah, but you know about that." He laughed unkindly, leading Scacciato into the room toward a panoply of bottles, gourds, and wine-skins, the residue of his night and day of celebration or mourning, whichever it was. "Come and have a good slosh with the man who has taken care of you all your life. Yes, I've done much for you, boy. I gave you a home in my kitchen when you had nothing and now I give you not only a beautiful wife - and she is a beauty - here." He thrust a bottle into Scacciato's chest. The young man took it and drank hard, saying to himself that if a bist could speak in between regurgitations, it would speak with the gravelly gorged voice of d'Oria. "Yes, not only a beautiful wife but a wonderful dowry which will keep you for the rest of your life so that you don't even need this land or my shops and storehouses in Genoa or anything from anybody. What say, young husband? Eh?"

Bring this to an end, he thought. Honestly, brutally, viciously, but quickly. "I was your slave, old merchant," he said, wrapping his palm around his chin as he often did when he needed courage to speak. "That's how you took care of me. As for your daughter, I will take her from you and I will take the dowry and with luck will never have to speak to you again." He took another drink as if to emphasize his desire to take things from d'Oria while treating him with contempt. "What do you say now, old man?"

"Ah you boy." d'Oria was not offended, perhaps had not even

comprehended. He grasped Scacciato more tightly and took a drink himself. "Now, I know you have no use for old Capece or anybody in the whole mansion, no more than I do. We are alike, you and I, both full of hate. But we must put it to use. Now with your brains and youth and with my money and guts, we could turn this place upside down. We could run this little island together."

"Stop this drivel, d'Oria. I won't in any way be in partnership with you."

"Well, let me help you anyway. I want to help you, you know that?" It seemed to Scacciato that d'Oria, beneath his contemptible personality, harbored some feelings of guilt about Scacciato's years of slavery. He was giving him his only child and a large part of his fortune but still he needed to give more. "Let me tell you about Emelia and what she will like for you to do."

Scacciato felt queasy but allowed him to continue.

"She likes to have her hair combed." He made motions like combing hair in the air. "Loves it, says it makes her tingle all down her back. And tweaking, she always likes a little tweak. When you're at dinner, reach up under her skirt, reach way up ..." Again he made the motions in the air. "... right between her legs and give her a little tweak right there while dinner is going on."

He grabbed the old man's neck like he had grabbed the dwarf - his first act of violence in seven years - and pushed him across the banquet table, then held him down and crawled on top of his chest. A thought flashed through his mind: you're always attacking dwarfs, first a physical dwarf and, in this case, a moral dwarf.

d'Oria was astonished; he genuinely did not understand the young man's anger. "What is this? I'm her father! What is wrong with you?" Scacciato could not speak but he could squeeze the old man's throat to make the voice a higher pitch. "You don't want to know how to make her happy? You don't want to know how to rub her places to make her smile?"

Scacciato began to bang d'Oria's head against the table.

"I only wish to make your wedding night a joy!"

Thunk, thunk, thunk, thunk. The sound of d'Oria's head against the table was immensely gratifying. Nightmare. You will make my wedding night a nightmare.

"This is what a father should do!" the drunken d'Oria tried to explain. "Who else should tell you these things?"

Several thoughts came to Scacciato all at once and clouded his desire to kill d'Oria. He realized that the old merchant probably thought his behavior was normal because, among his friends and acquaintances, it was normal. He also remembered the urgent need he felt to be outside in the woods, away from people. Finally, he recalled that touching Guasparrino d'Oria filled him with disgust and nausea. He let him drop on to the table. The old man was speechless, confused, and terrified.

Not yet, Scacciato thought. It is not yet time for this. He did not understand what his mind told him but he could not disobey it. As he looked down at d'Oria, who was still at his mercy, he believed that he could grasp the neck again and with long powerful fingers continue to squeeze until the oafish mouth could say no more, could tell no more lies, squeeze until the vacuous little eyes popped from their sockets and rolled down his hands, across the table, and on to the floor where they would make a sound like "splat" and lie there never to leer again. But his mind screamed. Stop. Hold, wait, prepare, but do not scramble your life over this. He backed off slowly, like a man cautiously lifting his foot from an insect to make sure it will not fly away, then slid to the floor, and stood looking at d'Oria.

He ran from the room, from the mansion, from the garden, into the thick woods that bounded the back side of the estate. He breathed heavily, gulping the morning air that was already warm with sunlight but tinged with a lingering cool from daybreak. He threw himself up a small rise and set out on a path he knew well, one he could follow without thinking, one he could have walked in his sleep. His legs took over, driving him through the forest, as if they knew his mind would be of no use in providing him direction.

He raced along in this bewitched manner, running his hands over his face or through his hair which began to stick out all over from the moisture in the air and the sweat on his scalp. He was twenty-two years old for this, his wedding day, but his confusion, his awe at his ability to contemplate murder, and his anger at himself because he had not committed it were the emotions of a boy, the kitchen slave salvaged from obscurity and hardship through the entangled vicissitudes of other people's lives.

Scacciato stopped for a moment and looked at his hands: powerful, nervous, murderous. At first he could not put into words or even put into thought the sensations coursing through his body. The memory of the dwarf and the feeling of hands wrapped around a throat filled him with a collection of emotions more unsettling than any he had ever known. Why had the attack on d'Oria seemed like the same event as the attack on the dwarf? Not similar, but the same. It was as if the two occurrences, seven years apart, were not subject to the usual constraints of time, space, and reason: they were the same event.

Suddenly a shudder like the death throes of the wretched bist produced an answer more terrifying than he could stand. He had felt an unnatural satisfaction when he was about to squeeze the life from another creature. He ran, blindly following his legs which took command again, flying to carry him far from his thoughts, far from his deadly, throbbing hands.

With the damp morning forest around him and the leaves and branches splashing dew in his face as he pushed through them, Scacciato began to calm down. It seemed to him that several ideas - too many - demanded his attention. He was full of hate, d'Oria was right about that. But did he hate them all? His father, certainly, for being a distant father and pompous politician and nothing more. d'Oria, yes he hated him. But Giusfredi? And also his wife and children? Emelia?

What of his mother? Cavriuola fascinated him; he thought again of her standing naked in the corridor. He recalled the futile effort he had invested trying to know her and remembered that she had left her children with the Nurse to go frolic with the deer, left them unprotected, and that he and Giusfredi had been kidnapped and indentured to d'Oria.

Then there was the question of what to do with his life, a question more important for a married man than for a child in his father's home. Become a priest? That was nonsense, even as a strategy for attaining power for other ends. He could never pretend well enough to pull it off. A soldier? Perhaps, but for what? For whom? A teacher, a scholar, an artist? Those pursuits were more suited to his natural temperament, but they sounded weak, passive, ineffectual, reminded him, in other words, of what he considered his flaws. He could manage the estate - no one else was doing it - or take over d'Oria's mercenary endeavors, but both ideas nauseated him.

What was left? Only the route that he could not consider for a single moment: to follow his father in governing Sicily. Even to engage in politics for the sake of opposing Arrighetto Capece, for the goal of defeating the man, seemed to Scacciato like giving in, playing his game with his rules, becoming, therefore, no better than his father.

The exhaustion of despair settled into his shoulders and back, as it did when he awoke from dreams of the bist. He stopped walking and leaned against a tree. He lost himself in the feel, the sound, and the smell of the woods. The dampness from the morning was gone, sunlight pushed through the treetops and warmed strips of the forest floor, things unseen scurried beneath the brush and made mysterious rustling noises. He felt alone finally and his mind went blank as he collapsed against the trunk of a tree.

The torment of thought ebbed. He felt released from his own questioning. After he had rested a few moments, he thought again and settled quickly and magically on the first conclusion of his adult life: There is a time to think, there is a time to act, and there is a time simply to keep going. This wedding day, he said calmly to himself, is a time to keep going.

Near noon, he strode toward home, for the first time in his life content with confusion.

III

He could hear voices as he left his sanctuary in the trees. The knot in his stomach reminded him of the impending monotony, an afternoon and evening filled with repeated conversations, most of them with strangers, the friends and cronies of his father and their families and all of their friends and cronies and families, the spiraling collection of people that appears at large more or less public weddings. There had been no social event of significance since King James arrived and, since Arrighetto Capece was at least the second most powerful man in Sicily, no one wanted to miss the wedding at the governor's mansion.

He looked through the low branches of a tree and watched for a moment. The garden was full of guests and servants, laughter, and toasting. He scrambled through the brush to the far side of the house, then ran to the nearest door, unseen and unaccosted. Reaching the third floor, he was relieved to find it quiet, apparently empty as the family joined their guests. Emelia, of course, had to be somewhere in the house; she would not be seen until just before the ceremony began. They would both wear white, almost indistinguishable in priest-like plain robes with gold trim. But only Giusfredi held anything like normal spiritual leanings. The rest all worshipped something - anyone could see it in their eyes - but it was something different for each one: power for Arrighetto Capece, childbearing for Spina, some animal deity for Cavriuola, money and drink for Guasparrino d'Oria, the future for Emelia, and for Scacciato some adolescent yet maturing notion of destiny or probity, some notion yet to be defined.

Still driven by the inevitability of unconsidered action, Scacciato hurried to his room and dressed. He believed that if he threw himself into the crowd downstairs, floated mindlessly in the waves of the occasion, trudged through the ceremony, he would not think consciously for a while

50

and thus relieve himself from the pain of recalling Guasparrino d'Oria's disgusting revelations and also allow his mind to work without interference, hoping that, just as an unwatched pot will boil, so an untended mind will find peace.

The nausea that threatened him on the landing as he looked out across the garden at the crowd eased when he forced himself to take the first step down. Soon he was caught up in the revelry, enjoying the attention, all of the brief, polite, and occasionally salacious remarks that people offer to one about to be married. It is working, he told himself. Being lost in this nonsense, this crush of congratulatory conversation, brings me a temporary peace. I will forget it all, forget my thoughts and wondering for the rest of the day. Later, tonight, or possibly tomorrow morning, I will think again.

He turned to accept another handshake and immediately thought: Grow up! That is what I must do! I must grow up! Then my life will be clear, then I will know what to do to free myself from the past, how to create my own story, find where my place is in this world. I am facing the challenges of manhood with the perspective of a boy. It is time now to grow up, wrestle this inchoate collection of urges and emotions and knowledge into a life. I will simply keep telling myself tonight to grow up, then tomorrow I can begin! He picked up the thread of conversation around him and joined in his own party, radiating peace and confidence, demonstrating a presence none of the guests or the family had ever seen before.

There were two hundred guests milling about the grounds, all squinting in the blinding sun. From the roof of the mansion, an observer would have seen a mass of moving colors sparkling in the June sunlight. Guests rotated around the individual members of the family so that there seemed to be five or six cogs that remained stable while continually changing wheels of human flesh and colored cloth circled them, the wheels oiled by the flowing of servants bearing drink and food, never stopping, linked to yet another machine of people in the kitchen, preparing and pouring without pause. Young servant boys there ran panting as Scacciato once had, reacting to each new order from a cook or server as soon as they finished obeying the previous order.

But the observer atop the mansion would have noticed also the union of man's cycle with that of the Earth: the burning of the sun and the cleansing of the summer zephyrs, the Earth working on itself to keep moving, to keep advancing without the power to know why, and at the same instant the purging and renewal of humans, marrying off another pair to carry on, the dying old not quite aware of their dying or their replacement, the inheriting young only vaguely and stupidly conscious of their succession. Perhaps the rooftop observer could detect the presence of a young man trying to grasp the meaning of it all. But perhaps not. Perhaps the observer would have been distracted, as everyone else was, by the collapsing of the throng away from the ground floor doorway, an involuntary stepping back as the bride, the deity of the day, stepped shyly into the windy sunlight.

Emelia was eighteen years old but, except for a few inches of height and slightly more colored features, she looked very much as she had when she first set foot in Sicily at age eleven. Her darkened hair, still uncut, framed her like curtains around a window. The guests looked upon her and saw two waves, one the auburn hair and the other the white robe, undulating as she walked. She presented to them an image not only of beauty but of importance, the importance of a child who knows that she is the center of attention and that she will be important in other ways, that men and children will somehow build elaborately constructed lives based on her, using her frailness as a miraculous foundation. She radiated that sense of impending strength, a readiness to accept her position.

A half-concealed smile on her face reminded the guests that she was still a child, likely as not to break into laughter at nothing. She stood for a few minutes greeting the people who surrounded her quickly, unsure of what she was supposed to do. Then Cavriuola reached her, looking more than ever like her natural mother, whispered to her, and led her by both hands through the crowd. They walked haltingly to a stone platform in the center of the garden directly in front of the blue-painted fountain. It was time for the wedding to begin.

Arrighetto Capece had made all the arrangements, including the selection of someone to perform the ceremony. They called the man Father Aram, although it was generally known that he was not with the church, any church. Capece could not bring himself to employ anyone remotely connected to the Papacy. He had fought too long against the secular schemes of the Pope. He felt vaguely excommunicated, as if the official ejection of King Frederick years before for failing to embark on a crusade had filtered down to him, as if by his loyalty to the line of Frederick he shared some shadow of that historic denunciation, that by his political stance he had forced the Pope (who may not have even known Capece's name) to excommunicate him in his heart if not publicly.

So instead of a church official, there was this "holy man" Father Aram, assuredly legal and legitimate as a bestower of marriage blessings (Capece himself would file a statement of marriage somewhere in the bowels of state, perhaps even have the King's seal affixed just for the hell of it), certainly religious in his appearance (a tall thin man with plain black shirt and pants, long black frock, brown sandals, bald head with only hoary grizzled fuzz to take the harshness away, pink face and lively dark eyes, peaceful smile which could belong only to a saint or an idiot), and carrying the right tool: a worn little bound volume with frayed stitching containing either sacred verses or ritual incantations which he must have known by heart since he never opened the volume.

Father Aram moved to the platform in the heavy steps of a tall man certain of his place. Rumors about him said that he was Moslem or Assyrian, that he was a renegade priest no longer recognized by the church, that he kept a small holy building up in the mountains filled with chickens and goats and caskets of wine. A small cadre of followers fed off him, mesmerized by his earthy wisdom. But none of that mattered. The governor had chosen him and he was in place, smiling at the air, clutching his little volume.

Scacciato unconsciously moved from idle socializing to the beginning of a serious ceremony uniting him with a young woman he had never bedded. His decision to shut off all thoughts except for his nonspecific plan to grow up had worked. Talking to strangers like the aristocrat he was, forging through the crowd to take his proper place, leaping into the traditional marriage; it all seemed right, things a grown person would do. The hatred and confusion still burned in the back of his mind but now more like something he knew would be there regardless of events, something to come back to, something apart from what he or anybody else did. He did not understand this collection of feelings and thoughts but he believed he was not making a big mistake.

Father Aram imitated a lawn statue as the family pushed through the crowd to form a semicircle around the wedding platform. Cavriuola and Emelia arrived first (custom dictated that the bride should wait for the groom and not the reverse). They stood to the right: Cavriuola looking directly at Father Aram with her cool, insane happiness, Emelia nervously laughing and glancing at the guests. Soon Giusfredi and Spina stood behind them with their children, none yet waist-high but all boisterous and using the wedding as an excuse to be more excited than usual, pausing in their fidgets only briefly when whacked on their heads by their mother, who never looked down or had to aim to hit the right one's crown and who never lost her smile or disturbed her husband's grip around her dough-like waist.

The fathers of the wedding couple, both besotted from a day's drinking that had begun with breakfast, were now sizzling in the sun like wine-soaked meat over a fire. They came from opposite directions through the throng with but one thought dominant in their minds: their child was about to marry the offspring of a pig.

Scacciato worked his way through the mob of strangers. All of them wanted to touch him, shake his hand, slap his back, squeeze his shoulder, reach out and at least feel his shirt to be a part of the event. He moved still blindly, unthinkingly, at peace, enjoying the feeling even though he knew it was temporary, as ephemeral as the joy of a peasant who drinks at the end of his week until he is conscious that his consciousness is disappearing as he sees for a moment both sunset and sunrise through the tavern door, believes at the same time that his troubles and pain and hunger and aching muscles are a thing of history and that he is doomed to live that pain and aching for the rest of his life until one day, sunrise and sunset are truly the same.

The crowd was dense around the platform. He had to use his hands to pry people apart to make room to walk. He could sense that others were trying to do the same thing, although he did not know that Arrighetto Capece was coming from the other side of the garden with food and wine stains on his ceremonial robes and sweat beads of anger and discomfort oozing down his wizened face. As he neared his destination, Scacciato could hear d'Oria behind and to his left. "Let me through, you bastards, I'm the father," he shouted repeatedly, not even stopping when he had reached the clearing and stood ten feet from his daughter, not even stopping when Father Aram raised his arm gently and put a finger across his lips or when Sctacciato and the rest of the family acknowledged his presence first with nods, then smiles, then waves, then stern looks. He stopped only after Arrighetto Capece burst from the opposite edge of the crowd, almost fell down, took up a solemn pose behind the right of his son and then, noticing with ineffable disgust who was making all the racket. He turned toward d'Oria and shouted "Shut up or die, you moron!"

The sound of scores of people attempting to stifle their laughter was like a stampede of cattle with their hooves bound in cloth: muted but thunderous at the same time. Father Aram brought it to an end by taking charge of the situation. "Are all the participants ready?" he asked. "Is everyone in place?" His reedy voice contrasted propitiously with the bass mumbling of the onlookers; it drew attention like a whistle, commanded that everyone realize that the previous act was finished and a new one was about to begin.

They loathed each other. To d'Oria, this ass-kissing blustering sycophant politician was what he could never be: important. Even as Capece had waited out fourteen years in a stone cell not wide enough or long enough to allow him to extend his legs while d'Oria was busily making fortunes in trade with all the freedom modern man can have, Capece was important in ways d'Oria would never be. Capece had taken him into his home, it is true, had given him a minor position so that he could call himself something more than a merchant, swapper of goods and coins, had created for him a situation in which he could abandon his enterprises and count his savings or continue to direct them from his island of retirement if he wished or even squander his accumulated wealth and simply live off the Governor, as long as he made little Emelia happy and therefore kept Scacciato occupied if not happy.

Capece had given d'Oria everything but importance. He had reduced him to ancillary status. He was free to go, of course. He could go back to Genoa to make more money and drink with his comrades, telling lies in the taverns and drunkenly buying women by the night. But he loved his daughter. She was all that was not common, vile, and empty in his life. If only he could stay here in Sicily, with her hawk-nosed little husband, and live with some decency, some importance, some respect.

This bear-man, this growler of orders who told him to shut up on the day - the very moment - of his glory, this imperious governor of Sicily prevented him from retaining any dignity at all. What could he do against the governor of Sicily?

Guasparrino d'Oria stood to the left and to the rear of Scacciato. Capece stood about ten paces to the right of d'Oria and behind his son, who was not aware that he had become a fulcrum of antipathy for two men in the autumn of their years. Would they have been there, hating each other, sticky and breathless in the early summer sun, if Scacciato had not existed? Just as a drunken man stumbles to the ground and beats his fist against the earth because it attacked his face, the two fathers could not accurately determine the causes of their discomfort. They only hated the sight of each other. How could they, lost in the heat of the moment, made volatile and emotional by a day's drinking, reason and calculate who was to blame?

Like any event, it was the product of countless causes, the end result of hundreds of human decisions, failures, blunders, strivings, dreams, schemings, accidents, misguided attempts to control a second of destiny. To trace the coming together of Capece and d'Oria at that instant might lead the inquisitive mind, the scholar of human events, back up a spider web of connected but unrelated phenomena; as he tried to follow each strand separately, he would know he was learning nothing. If he tried to follow all the strands at once, he would go mad, find himself dangling like a giant insect across the web, flailing and twisting with no purpose but escape, no wiser except for his fear of untangling the reasons for any occurrence, hoping only to extricate himself by promising his god never to raise his eyes again and ask "Why this?"

Scacciato tried to focus on Father Aram's rambling ceremony but he was gradually becoming aware of the tension behind him. His mind quickly flooded with a sense of panic, but perhaps only the panic which millions of men and women feel during an important ritual of commitment whether it is marriage or joining an army or a religious order or any of the other ways man tries to connect with something beyond himself. Then another thought occurred: he was acting without the tedious and agonizing consideration he usually gave to matters of far less import than this. He also felt a vague uneasiness about the renegade churchman and his jumble of prayers and mumbling (phrases attached to a speech with no more meaning to them than barnacles on a ship's bottom), the sense of impending catastrophe behind his back which he did not want to identify, the realization that he had never kissed his bride, that this person about to be his wife had a mind which he really did not know.

He turned to her but the seething face, thick beard, and massive shoulders of his father just beyond Emelia dominated his field of vision. He faced Father Aram again, then slowly, almost imperceptibly, turned his head back to the right, stopping at each fraction of an inch to be sure that Capece was not visible, finally catching the beginning of Emelia's face at the edge of his field of vision, so straight up and down that not even her nose was visible first; the forehead, the nose, and the chin all arrived at the same time. At that point, he moved his head and eyes even more slowly until he could see her entire face and about an inch behind her hairline on the side of her head. He froze there, knowing that if he moved his eyes even slightly, the picture of his bride - child-like, soft, pretty, someone he honestly would try to love - would be blasted from his mind by the sight of his father, huge, grotesque, hard, reeking of power and wine, someone who would remain forever a stranger, and no one he could ever love.

I will finish this, he thought. I will play this out. And why not? To have a lovely wife is no problem, nothing to complain about. It is not surrender to the world of my father or to the past. This woman is my doing. So what if it is slightly connected to the past, my consolation from d'Oria for having been his slave? Our being husband and wife will be our doing, no one else's. And I will continue to learn, to write my treatise, to overcome the past and the life of our fathers, even though we must for now live on this land and their fortune. This is, in fact, the first major act of my life and the first of her life as well. Now we are no longer children, he thought, and can never be again. This is important! This is good! And it is mine, not his!

This frenzy of self-congratulation loosened Scacciato's control or perhaps it emboldened him. In either case, he relaxed his neck and allowed it to shift further to the right, far enough to see Arrighetto Capece's eyes, already red, turn a murderous eggplant color. For during the interval in which Scacciato had convinced himself that his marriage was an act of independence, Capecce had convinced himself that the world would be an extraordinary and delightful place, a seraphic lodge, an Eden of unspoiled tranquility, if Guasparrino d'Oria became dead.

Capece did not stop to analyze his hatred; he never examined or questioned strong emotions. Indeed, the desire to destroy d'Oria sprang from assumptions so basic to the governor of Sicily that he could not have questioned them. He told himself that only those who fight and struggle for domination, for rule, for order, truly live in this world while the others - the churchmen, the artists, the thinkers - merely pass the time, whittle away the years pretending they are alive.

And beneath the churchmen, the artists, and the thinkers, several levels down the human hierarchy, living off the world, leeching from others, taking but not giving, are the merchants, creatures who are all arms and fingers - no heart, no mind, no soul, no guts - octopeds of greed who seek an empty puissance: wealth for the sake of wealth. Those merchants had fueled his battalions and fed his island treasury but they were the evanescent pillars who forgot his name when the wind blew another direction, who sold their arms to the Pope, to the French, to whoever had money to buy while Arrighetto Capece fumed in prison and learned to hate them, completely and vengefully. Now a merchant was a part of his household through a quirk, an accident, an obligation that Capece endured because he had a second son who had suffered and now was free, deserving a bride and capital of his own. But the beauty and curse of wine is that it reduces such complexities to simple questions with inelectable answers. "Endure?" Capece muttered to himself. "Must I endure this drunken parasite? Of course not!" he answered himself, suddenly flinging himself at the despised d'Oria.

Behind Scacciato's back, the two heavy men were suddenly wrestling on the ground. The crowd backed away and the members of the family stepped toward the platform, horrified, despondent over the interruption of the ceremony. Scacciato, however, did not move. He clasped his hands in front of him and looked straight ahead as if he could not hear his father growling the words "son of a pig" or his future father-in-law breathlessly answering with a phrase not intelligible to the listeners.

He did not step forward, even when the two men - both too old, too hot, too heavy, too drunk for this adolescent escapade on the ground - rolled into the backs of his legs. He planted himself more firmly, knowing that in time the warrior Capece would subdue the slovenly merchant and step away, come to his limited senses. Besides, he told himself, this is my day, not theirs. If they want to spend their time rolling in the dirt, that's fine. They can spend the day rolling in shit or rolling in hell or rolling off the face of the earth for all I care.

"Continue," Scacciato commanded, looking at the flustered Father Aram but addressing the whole company. At first they did not believe him but when his rigid look did not change, they began to move back into place, each thinking, each responding to Scacciato's order in their own way.

Father Aram: The boy is right, it is his wedding, it's up to him to say when it goes and when it doesn't go.

Emelia (stepping back to her place, proudly): It is true our fathers despise each other but I cannot stop now to worry about that or extricate my father from another mess any more than Scacciato can stop to curse the father he detests. I am his wife and it is time to behave as his wife. Perhaps this sharp-nosed morose young man will be all right. Perhaps he is worthy of love and respect. Furthermore (with a soft laugh that made the others turn toward her), it is pretty funny, these two old men drunk and scuffling in the dirt. At least they cannot hurt each other.

Giusfredi: A good man, my brother. A good man to take charge like that. But is it only his way of proclaiming his distate for our father? Perhaps I should go to Capece's aid anyway. Perhaps it is my duty as the first son. But here is my Spina stepping back into place with our children around her like the petals of a flower. I will stand beside her where I am happy, not wrestle in the dirt where I will be unhappy.

And Spina: The old bastard never lets go of his passion and his ferocity. His flame never goes out. But now is not the time to go to him. It is time to stand with my Giusfredi and keep the children from getting hit by a flailing arm.

Cavriuola (leaping into position next to Emelia): These children understand what is important here today. Not too old bucks tearing antlers but this beginning, Scacciato and Emelia leaving behind their childhoods, leaving their past grunting in the dirt where it belongs. Capece can fight his own wars. Scacciato can fight his own wars. There was no war on the isle of Ponza where I lived in exile because of that old man. There were only soft gentle deer.

"Yes, continue," she said, assuming her position as the only parental figure present and able to stand up.

Father Aram hurried through his unique ceremonial speech, pausing periodically when the grunting of the fighting fathers became too loud. The crowd maintained a respectful silence except for an occasional whisper of encouragement to one or another of the fighters. The marriage was like a complex sweaty machine. It consisted of three concentric half-circles (one moving, the other two stationary) and a critical gear in the center. The guests formed the thick outer rim. Inside them the two warriors formed the second layer with their constant rolling which forced the onlookers to leave them enough space for a score of men. The innermost half-circle (the wedding party of five adults and Spina's orbiting children) faced the center point of the contraption: Father Aram reciting his verses, politely skipping over the sections which would normally require participation by either the father of the bride or the father of the groom. The wedding ended before the fight did.

Scacciato turned and kissed his bride, looked curiously into her eyes, and began to wonder what he had done. But not for long.

It was a tradition, they said, to separate the newlyweds and get them drunk, but no one could explain whose tradition it was, nor could anyone remember doing it before. But that did not matter. Like any idea conceived and gestated in a crowd, it sprang from a casual comment quickly forgotten and later unattributed, grew into a certainty, an axiom, an unavoidable obligation, and drove its servants - the wedding guests - with the power of religious fervor. Two small groups informally charged with their duty before the ceremony emerged; each snatched a newlywed from the arms of the other and spirited them to opposite corners of the garden. The rest of the company wandered around talking, toasting, laughing, alternating between the two small groups, watching the friendly inundation of the bride and groom. They completely forgot the two old men, now panting desperately on the ground in a pile and striking each other with arms of lead and fists of straw.

When they first picked him up by the arms and carried him away from his bride, Scacciato hated them for it, vowing to get revenge some day. After a few moments in the arms of these guests invited by his father - the groom himself had no friends - he gave in to the event. And the men poured the wine, again and again, until it spilled from Scacciato's gulping mouth, until his white wedding tunic oozed red, until they could release his arms and legs, knowing that they were useless to him.

Much later: faces were liquid, cups of wine were thoughts, genius hid under the rocks of the garden path. Son and father in the dirt one hundred feet apart, each wrestling with a fatuous mortality taken the form of an unctuous merchant for the father, pebbles with suction grippers for the son. Leg as twigs, snapping under the weight of gravity, flung Scacciato against the stone wall of a flower bed, upending dozens of yawning faces that swelled in howls jowl to jowl, their chins elongated then widened into bulbous swarms, connecting like ripples in a pond, becoming massed, inseparable: it was a giant's face laughing at him, gnashing yellowed teeth around his legs (legs wiggling like worms above his head), eyes flashing with derision, nightmare and exultation become one. He reached for the face, pulled himself up on the laughter, stood crouched briefly, then dove for pearls into the swirling red petunias. The snickering of the guests - and dirt - thundered in his ears.

Where is my friend? he asked himself. I had a friend here and that's why all these people came, to see me and my friend, but where is she now? Maybe she is under this rock or maybe under that one. As the young bridegroom proceeded on his knees down the path, ideas began to come back to him, exposing themselve through the drunken haze.

Grow up, he thought. That was what I was going to do. Grow up. He said this to himself as he dragged his besotted body up to a stone bench but then forgot it briefly when several men his father's age surrounded him and, laughing robustly, held his unresisting head back and poured more wine into him.

Ah yes, growing up, he thought when they had left him. I wonder if this is growing up? It must be because all of these grown-up people are doing this to me. (His usual iron logic had rusted into flakes.) A time to think and a time to act and a time to ...a time to do this. Let me stand up and do this.

He was drunk enough to stand up again finally. He found the nearest cluster of people, took a bottle from someone's hands and drank fiercely, then talked vociferously for half an hour until he was alone again. No one had understood a single sentence he uttered.

Where is she, he asked himself? Maybe that is her over there, hanging from that tree limb, that white fluttery thing dangling in the moonlight. When do I get to grow up?

He finished the rest of his wine, walked with a determined but slopppy gait toward what he believed to be Emelia rippling in the night air under a tree limb, and fell face first into the shrubbery, ignored by the few remaining guests.

IV

He awoke on a padded settle, his head bent against one wooden arm, his feet propped on the arm at the other end. He had slept in his wedding suit soaked with wine. He rubbed his eyes, the stinging embers of the first alcoholic stupor of his life. After a minute, he rolled over on his side and surveyed the room. The settle where the rowdy guests had dumped him occupied the center of an interior wall with the corner fireplace at Scacciato's feet. He focused on the mantle over the fireplace and slowly moved his eyes around the room, holding his gaze momentarily at each spot before moving on to the next, as a trembling man would attach himself to each new object before fully releasing his grip on his previous source of support. The candles, nearly spent, reflected off the windows of the outside wall. Long single panes ran from near the ceiling to waist height. Through the near window he could see that the night was starless and still as a tomb.

In the center of the room to his left were two thick-cushioned chairs with a small table between them, a place for husband and wife to talk, be alone together before bedtime. He looked beyond these to the wide high doorway in the far corner next to the darkest window. Not enough light came in from outside to illuminate what was beyond the doorway, nor did the candles cast their light that far. He knew that the rest of their suite of rooms must be through that opening and, now becoming clearheaded as well as sentimental about his new wedded state, he imagined hmself and Emelia living in these rooms, growing together, racing through the mundane events of their life, busy, content, adult. He imagined himself behaving as a normal man, a husband, a father, throughout each day, through dinner, into the evening, then stealing madly down to the second floor after Emelia was in bed, back to his small study, mysteriously locking himself in, secretly writing his treatise, and making plans into the late hours like a man living a shadow life that is all his own.

Along the wall opposite him stood a long chest, only three feet high but as long as the entire room. On top of it were things that he could not identify in the darkness or perhaps because he had never shared a room with a woman. These were women's things, magic and arcane, little artifacts of womanhood, clothing, figurines, colored bottles, carvings, some papers, tiny ornate boxes booby-trapped to destroy the man who clumsily opened them.

The smell of Emelia filled the room - and him - with anticipation. To be a part of this was to learn something he did not know, something the priests and desiccated scholars could not teach him. He shook himself from his state of wonder and turned his head back and to the left as far as he could without getting up from the settle. He could see clearly only a tall candle stand with one low-burning candle trying to cover its corner of the room. Just at the edge of his vision, he saw the side of a bedpost and a piece of the canopy that hung down the post. The bed! His bed! Their bed! He flung himself off the settle to his feet and into the center of the room. He thought he saw her (his wife now) bedraggled, damp with wine, and thrown to the bed, but only for an instant before he blacked out and hit the floor, crashing like a stack of plates.

When his eyes opened he saw Emelia's face, gentle, young, and spinning in the blackness.

"Have you hurt your head?" she asked, touching his temple. A thousand shivers rattled through his body like it was a peasant's ancient cart crossing a ford.

"Not too badly." He tried to sound convincing, but his voice trembled. He sat up and looked at her but he was still unable to distinguish features. She rubbed his temples gently and his mind became clearer even though his vison was still blurred.

When they stood up, a piercing pain rose to the ceiling of his skull but as he saw Emelia smile he found the strength to counter the discomfort left from the day of forced drinking.

"We should get out of these nasty clothes," she whispered.

He stood in front of her with his dark recessed eyes moist and mad. He pulled his tunic over his head and threw it on the floor. Emelia giggled. He peeled his pants off and she laughed out loud.

Confused and embarrassed, he pulled her to him. They kissed and he understood: the same bubbling undertone - almost the purr of a cat - that was there when she laughed and was still there when the laughter was gone. In seconds, he undressed her and flung the two of them into the bed.

He remembered for an instant something the Nurse had told him several years before. He had been brooding in her third floor room, boring her with his adolescent sadness. "Past is past, little Scacciato," she had said as she always did. Then she added: "There are only two ways of living in this world, Scacciato, and you must choose one of them. You can live in joy and your life will race by. It will be over before you know it. Or you can live in gloom and sadness and life will be with you a very long time."

"Nonsense," he had told her as he stalked out of the room. Gloom prolong life? Joy hasten death? Yet now he saw joy and death beneath him in the bedcovers and he made his choice instantly, even though he heard the years begin to flutter away with her soft laughter.

"You are a strange young man, Scacciato," she said as she put her arms around his back. "I do not know you even though we have been under the same roof for seven years. I am not sure if it's possible but I will try to know you."

"I do not know what will become of us, Emelia. I don't know how long I can stay in my father's house."

"I know." She ran her fingers up and down his back.

He looked into her clear eyes, aware of the rest of her - her hair a long veil, her body still that of a child, her face unremarkable but also unforgettable - and saw a reflection of himself. There is the man, he thought. Perhaps he has been there all along.

They threw themselves into lovemaking like pigeons going after crumbs, with the same passion and the same ineptitude. Amidst all the pecking and cooing they sometimes made each other feel good; at intervals just as frequent, they scratched, poked, elbowed, bit too hard, squeezed the wrong spot. Emelia felt a rawness developing on the skin beneath her breasts from Scacciato's beard. She discovered a fascination for squeezing his hip bone - exciting for her, nearly excruciating for him. But they enjoyed, they played, they laughed. Emelia repeated often the phrase "plant me" which made neither sense nor romance to her new husband. He humored her and began to murmur "I will plant you, my Emelia."

For most of an hour they frolicked with no thoughts but love and play. For another half an hour they tried in vain to consummate their play with something more serious. It would not happen. He rolled over on his side and hated it. His new bride was for the time being impenetrable.

Emelia lay on her back still and quiet; he missed her laughter already. He thought that she was thinking of their predicament but it was soon clear that her mind was on something else. She turned to face him and with a trace of a smile whispered: "Do you want to hear something funny?"

"Something funny?" It hardly seemed the time.

"Come. I've done it before. It will make you laugh!" She rolled out of bed, took his hand, and yanked him to his feet. She pulled him across the room through their chambers before he could say no or stop and led him into the dark hallway. Only seconds before he was angry in bed; now he tiptoed naked behind his wife, watching her swirling hair tickle her bare backside, catching a glimpse through the window of the night becoming dense and rainy.

Their suite of rooms was at the rear side of the third floor, directly above Scacciato's study and his buffer zone of empty rooms on the second floor. The Nurse stayed in a small space barely more than an alcove, right in the middle of the third floor. In all the time she had lived there with one third of a mansion to herself, she had never used more than that tiny room, meticulously keeping the rest of the floor both clean and uninvaded.

It only took them a minute to tiptoe down the hall and into the vacant room next to hers, but years later he would remember it as a long symphony of radiant images and ineffable joy. It was nothing, of course, only Emelia sliding gently down the hall, almost disappearing in the dark passage but reappearing as they passed each window, reappearing to him as something not altogether mortal but ethereal and magic when the dim starlight painted her hair, her back, her behind, and her legs with lambent coloring.

She crouched against the wall in the empty room, barely containing her laughter as she drew him down beside her. Squatting low, his penis touched the floor. "Shush," she whispered, although he had said nothing. With her finger across her lips, she put her ear to the wall and bade him to do the same. He remembered the Nurse's lover, old Anglico, when he heard the sounds coming through the wall. The two old people were very loud, either grown a little deaf or just used to having the floor to themselves. Apparently, the bed was pushed against the wall and they were making love only inches from their young audience. Scacciato could hear groans and sighs and sibilant liquid sounds. And then some words: "Plant me, my gardener," the Nurse said in the voice that had been his mother's voice for fourteen years. "Plant me again and again. I am your garden tonight, old man. Plant me, my gardener."

"Perhaps," Scacciato whispered, ignoring Emelia's frantic shushing and waving of hands, "it is not so bad to grow old." She had to cover her mouth and run from the room almost choking on the stifled laugh. He caught up with her and took the lead this time. Just as the pregnant mugginess finally delivered its rain, he pulled her into bed. It stormed outside and in the bed for the rest of the night: day-like flashes of stunnning light, deep shuddering roars, uncontrolled wetness falling everywhere, leaving no crevice dry. At the dawn of exhaustion, soaked, wilted, and reborn like the earth outside, Scacciato said to himself: "I will always be the Outcast but maybe ... maybe I will not have to be alone." They slept through the new day, splayed across the bed, husband and wife, the Outcast and his bride.

V

The freakish winter wind blew fear through the mansion. No one remembered a colder night nor could they think of a worse time for it to happen. The powerful wind and the weakened Emelia screamed; the family cringed and waited. Scacciato squeezed the window sill at each of her screams, thinking that the child must soon come or his wife would die. Each blast of the wind rattled the window but could chill him no more. The cold in his bones was disorienting, painful, so pervasive that it could not get worse.

"What if she dies?" He spoke to himself out loud. Here in the sitting room he was only footsteps from their bedroom where Emelia lay. Between her cries, one of the women might hear him talking to himself but he did not care. "What if she dies?" he asked again, the question frosting on the inside of the window. The wind answered with an indifferent moan.

An explosion of rain came without warning, then quit after a few seconds. "This night is strange," he said, feeling the moisture on the pane. "This weather is bizarre, even for February. Perhaps it is the proper kind of night for the son of an outcast to be born." A wave of rain came again but quit as soon as the first drops hit the ground.

"Gloom," he mumbled. "Why should birth be a time of gloom and bodily terror? What Creator dreamed this up? What lunatic?" He looked up at the sky, now beautifully silver but torn open and bleeding by the wind . "If you are not a lunatic, strike me dead!" he commanded. "If you are there at all, strike me dead!" Nothing happened. "Fables and fairy tales," he said, looking down at his long hands clutching the window sill.

The sitting room was his refuge for the night. Spina and Cavriuola were with Emelia, as were several servants and one haggard midwife, a toad-faced woman with scarred and knotty skin who terrified Scacciato with one look. He wanted to throw her out but he could not bring himself to cross her, only partly because she was reputed by the local villagers to cast spells on people who annoyed her.

Giusfredi was not yet home from his council work, d'Oria had passed out after supper, and Capece was absent, a fact notable only because he had been inexplicably hanging around the mansion during the evenings in recent months. Occasionally one of the women came out to Scacciato in the nearly dark room to report that "she is a brave girl" or that "things are going as well as can be expected" and once that the midwife warned him to stop scowling or the child would be born with a split lip.

"She's having the child too soon," he said for the tenth time that night. "He's at least a month early. Surely he will never live. Perhaps she was already - no." He remembered their wedding night. "No, it is ours. Why did we have to be so fertile? If only she had not come with child right away - we've not been married a year - she could have been a little older, a little stronger."

He gripped his upper arms as if to pass some of his strength to her in the next room, to give her and the child the benefit of his exercise and training, his secret regimen of running, leaping, and lifting that filled his mornings. They said it was miraculous how his body had blossomed since his marriage and he smiled at them, telling no one that it came from hours of hard painful work in a clearing in the forest when he was supposed to be overseeing the work of the peasants. No one knew that he ran around the pond a hundred times a day, practiced relentlessly with his sword against the defenseless trees, and lifted heavy logs over his head.

He turned his back to the window and shuddered when the damp wind beat at his shoulders as if the panes of glass were not even there. He leaned back and looked vaguely into the room. A massive mahogany sideboard lined the wall next to the bedroom, the fireplace and umber-colored mantle filled the inner wall, and several of Emelia's paintings — landscapes, animals, and one unsuccessful attempt to capture Cavriuola — decorated the far side of the room. He turned to look at the paintings, barely visible in the light from the small candle on the mantle, but he could not bear it. He felt death in the house, believed that someone would die on this night, and he could not look at the lively evidence of Emelia's year as his wife.

"What a year it's been," he said, his voice rattling like a skeleton through the lonely room. "Not even a year yet. My father is still fighting, still trying to wipe the papal ooze from the boots of Sicily, never quite finished, never fully in control even though King James gives him all the pathetic soldiers he wants. He will never be rid of fighting. There will always be enemies for men like Capece. But I must wonder for our sake ..." He looked at the closed door again. "There must some day be some kind of peace for our island, some stability. Perhaps I will have to do it or perhaps there will only be peace when Capece is gone." His mind raced down a rich vein of imagination but he pulled it back.

"We have been happy enough, Emelia and I. It is for the best that we are together, though I cannot seem to take her completely into my confidence. I cannot share my treatise with her, of course. That is still my own. So is my dream of clipping Capece's wings. At least the details are mine alone. And the daily training, the balancing of my body with my mind, the physical preparation for my contest with the past or whatever it shall be, that I keep secret from her as well, although she can see the results. Damn it! What do I share with her? The child, of course. This human threatening to be real. But what else? Surely there is more? Love-making, yes, some talk about what we have both learned over the years, some daily chatter and household routines. That is so much?" He softened inside, listening for her cries, which had diminished for a few moments.

"That is much. It is necessary, it is valuable. Isn't that exactly what I never had as a child, the wonderfully reassuring routine of family? Yes, it has made a difference, the being there, the regularity of it, the certainty and definition of so many little things, that my wife sits next to me at the dinner table, for example. It is that definition of my daily life which enables me to pursue something larger and more important."

He stalked across the room as if with a purpose, then returned to the window the same way. The walk shifted his thoughts to another topic. He addressed the bitter cold outside. "There is never long in this life before I have to ask myself what next. Here only months ago I thought that I should know something about my life before I married but I did not so I went ahead. Which was good. Yes. The dreams stopped, just went away like magic. No more wretching little bists in my sleep. But they came back!"

He smashed his fist on the wall and framed the window with his long muscular arms.

As he stretched his fingers out, he resembled a giant frog hanging on a garden wall. "Just this last month it started back, began creeping into my mind at night like a vile ghost, hideous, ominous. Why? Damn you, Little Vision, why? I have made something of my life. Not something for ever but for now. I've taken over the estate and basically run it all by myself. I oversee the work and deal with the tradesmen and the brokers and the bankers. We did quite well this year, in fact. But of course *he* controls the profits." He thought he heard snickering somewhere in the room but when he whirled around there was no one visible, only the shadows. From the adjoining room, Emelia shouted "Jesus!" and he wondered if she was calling for Jesus to help or if she was blaming him for this atrocity. He looked at her paintings on the wall, bright and cheerful pictures, and wondered if she would live to paint more.

"So what now? Is this the success I'm destined for? To run this estate and make us all more wealthy so I can provide my family ..." He choked and had to stop while he thought of the new one tearing his way into the cold winter of life, leaving bloody fragments of his mother's body and his father's mind in his wake. One of three women dies in their first childbirth, they had told him, one of three was the midwife's experience. "What a ghastly record," he mumbled. "And she sings her own praises and dares to appear again. But the believers sing the praises of their God and surely his record is no better." He looked at the closed door, tried to see through it. "And here is another one who may waste away here and make no more sense of it than the rest of us."

Never had he felt such despair, futility, and helplessness, not even as a kitchen slave. He wanted to push his fist through the window; the senselessness of the act, not the fear of pain, kept him from it. He would only earn himself a bloody stump.

He rubbed his hands together and felt the cold pane. Then, "I've got it!" he shouted, startling himself. He waited a few seconds to see if anyone came from the bedroom. "I will change this little world of ours. I will turn it inside out. I will conquer it, destroy it, rebuild it, make it mine in some way. That is what I will do." A long, loud cry of frenzied pain came from the next room. "Those things I can do," he said quickly, "though

I cannot prevent even one minute of her pain."

He jumped when Spina opened the door. Light from the many candles in the busy bedroom shattered the darkness of the sitting room and momentarily froze Spina in silhouette in the doorway. He advanced with the question "Is it over?" trembling on his lips but before he could ask a new crescendo of screams from the next room told him that Emelia fought on.

Spina stood framed in the doorway for a moment. Her hair was put up as if for a party but strands fell around her face, secret whispers of black violating the milky skin. She wore a thin flowered gown and over it a heavy woolen robe of dark brown, both parted slightly at her chest, belted at the waist, and touching the floor, neither able to conceal her fascinating shape. He was glad when she spoke because it stifled a disturbing quiver of lust he felt for her.

"Scacciato," she said, as if there was nothing wrong, as if there was no danger, as if the murderous cold was not at that moment clawing at the mansion walls. "It won't be long now. You will be a father soon, and Emelia is going to be just fine."

He stepped close to her and touched her arm; he could not help himself. "Aren't you needed in there?" She closed the door behind her as he asked, "Shouldn't you be with her to ... do something?"

"Not at all," she laughed, putting her arm around his back. "They have all the hands in there they can possibly use. Besides, it is mostly Emelia's work now. Come, let's sit and talk." She squeezed his waist as she led him to the high-backed chairs in the center of the room. "Cavriuola, the Nurse, and the mid-wife are with her. They will see that all goes well."

She sighed as she relaxed into the chair. Scacciato sat tense on the edge of his seat with his knees almost touching hers. He looked anxiously at her face, noticed that she looked tired, thought how rare it was to see Spina look tired. He felt a dozen questions whirling in his head but he could not put them into words. "Well?" he finally asked.

"Well what?" she smiled. "The child will be born soon, Emelia will be fine, and you will all live happily ever after. You can stop worrying, Scacciato." She settled further into her chair as she spoke, spreading out to fill the available space, as a dog in the summertime eases into a hole he has dug to keep cool.

His mind locked in incomprehension; he could not speak. He looked at her, stared at her, observed her as he had first observed Little Vision, believing that she had something to tell him or that she knew something that he should know. Nothing happened.

"And what was the outcome of the name debate?" Spina asked. She broke the silence without ever realizing that Scacciato was waiting, expecting some revelation, something more serious than simple conversation.

"Satan," he said.

"Scacciato," she said, covering her laugh with her hands. "Sometimes I think my brother-in-law is a madman. Really. What have you decided? Or have you decided? You know, Arrighetto Capece would love for you to give him a son with his name."

"I would rather rip off my arms than give him that. Why haven't you and Giusfredi given him a little Arrighetto? You have had ample opportunity."

She did not mind the reference to her fertility; it was a standard item of conversation in the household. "That is not what he wants from me." she said softly. "But he would want that from you."

"Then he will continue to want it. I will give him nothing, especially not the name of my child."

"We're a little touchy about names, aren't we?"

Scacciato scowled and turned his head. "I'm a little touchy about assholes."

"Why do you hate him so?"

"He's a miserable excuse for a human being," he said, the speech in his head always ready. "People are only scenery to him, his family bit players, Sicily, for all his talk of glory and tradition, the boards of a stage. They are all toys that he uses to play his child's game of power and self-adulation. Deep down, nothing means anything to Capece but Capece. If he had not been so immersed in his politics, my mother and brother would not have been sent alone into exile. I would not have been born an outcast, we would not have spent all the years apart, growing up strangers. We might have been a family. Even now, we are only background to him, part of the position he holds. He does not love my mother or even try to get close to her or try to understand her. He treats Giusfredi like a servant and he looks the other way when I'm around.

He's a beast."

She said nothing for a minute, although Scacciato could not tell if she was thinking, digesting his diatribe, or simply waiting. "You must admit ... Much of what you say is true but surely you must admit that he is full of life, he is interesting. Unlike most people, he is truly alive."

"I have noticed." He refused to elaborate.

"And the rest of us? Do you hate the rest of us as well?"

"I do not hate you, Spina." He was not sure if he was being honest now. "And Giusfredi. Sometimes I feel sorry for Giusfredi but I do not hate him. As for my mother ... I do not know. She is in her own world now, a happy world as far as I can tell. Do I hate her for that? Should I hate her for wandering off to play with deer and allowing Giusfredi and me to be stolen into slavery? Or should I hate Capece that much more for putting her in that position in the first place?"

"Well, at least I am glad that you do not hate Giusfredi." She seemed relieved to think about her husband for a moment.

"No. Giusfredi has never done me any harm." An idea flashed through his mind but he could not act upon it yet. It would have to wait.

"You worry me sometimes, Scacciato." She squinted her eyes as Capece often did. "You worry us all. One stands next to you and feels uncomfortable, as if you might turn our world upsidedown."

"Ah, but that is my aim," he said. "Not this world, our little mansion here, although that may go in the process. I believe that the world as we know it will not last very much longer. I believe that there will be and must be a time when kings and popes and nobles are gone. When the man, the family, the village will dominate. It will happen in time but the men like Capece who continue to wrap us in their webs of politics simply delay that time. I would like very much to change that."

"The man? The family? The village? What can they do against the power of kings and governors?" Her face lost its relaxed air of acceptance; the muscles tightened in confusion and fear. She pulled her robe around her more tightly to resist the chilling wind that even the stone walls could not keep out.

"Can't you see, Spina?" He edged further out of his chair and put his hand on her leg for emphasis. She did not notice; she was impaled on his eyes, which had become wider and supernaturally focused on some obsession that he now hurled like a javelin from deep in his soul, through his icy glare, and into her gentle face, leaving her frosted and stabbed.

The words started pouring out on the frightened woman just as they had splattered across the pages of his treatise night after night. "We are riding in a carriage that is going to collapse, Spina. The wheels are still on the axles but they are held in place only by our weight, by all the fat and baggage we carry with us. The wheels are slipping out from under us and soon one will go, then another and another and the whole contraption will come crashing to earth. And while we lie there on the ground, while we struggle to pull ourselves out of the rubble with our pathetic possessions in our hands, do you know who will be standing there watching us?"

"No," she whispered.

"The peasants. And do you know what they will do?"

"What?" She only formed the word on her lips, making no sound.

"Piss on us."

Spina gasped; she seemed to hold her breath while Scacciato stared at her with crazed eyes. They sat uncomfortably for several minutes. She did not want to breathe or look at him or speak. He gloated silently for having unnerved her, then began to feel uneasy himself.

Why did I bother to tell her all of that? he thought. She does not want to know, has no desire to understand. I have only made her scared and she will learn nothing from it. Fear can be useful but in this case it is simply pointless misery. And what have I gained from this? A few moments of distraction? The joy of watching my brother's wife twitch like a beheaded chicken? I do not dislike her enough to enjoy that. And she only came in here to help me, to pass some of the time while we wait. Wait! While we wait for my child to be born! I had forgotten!

"What is going on with Emelia? It's been very quiet in there. Shouldn't you go and see?"

It was the kindest thing he had ever done for Spina. As she blurted "My, oh yes" and strained out of the chair, he could see relief oozing from her face, from her entire body. They walked to the door together and he heard Emelia again although he could not be sure if she actually had been quiet for a few minutes or if the intensity of the conversation simply had blotted her out.

"I just want to say this," Spina said, with her hand on the door. "I know that you are more learned and more ... more deep than I will ever be but I believe that you are wrong. Things are as they are for a reason and things will stay as they are for that same reason. Perhaps not forever but ... at least as long as we will live." She stared at him, imploring him not to argue, then quickly hurried into Emelia's bedroom.

Scacciato rubbed his hands together as he returned to the window. He wrapped his arms across his chest and covered his shoulders with his hands. In the excitement of explaining himself to Spina, he had forgotten the cold, just as he had forgotten Emelia.

How strange that ideas can banish the earth and people from my mind, he thought. That is probably why I like to think so much. Suddenly he felt sure of himself, free of confusion and uncertainty, as if expressing his thoughts out loud to Spina had clarified them to himself.

He believed that he could see his life before him all at once, not in detail, not with regard to trivial particulars of place or circumstance, but in its form and structure, like seeing the frame of a house without yet seeing its walls and windows and doors; he could see the frame of the house that would be his life. He closed his eyes and saw Capece in ruins at his feet. He saw the frightening birth in the next room as only a memory and his grown child embarking on a wonderful and interesting life. He saw Emelia strong, healthy, and active again. He saw himself moving through the lives of other men, changing them, leaving them breathless, swamped by his power and importance. He saw Capece in ruins at his feet. Then like a ghostly wind, a cold shiver of shame spread across his back and shoulders. He was a kitchen slave again, abandoned by a father who cared more for politics than for family, misplaced by a mother who preferred her children to have four legs and hooves. He was small and insignificant, small and alone and ashamed. Weakened and weighted down, he rested his head against the frosted window. He did not know that he would sleep, did not realize at first that he had been asleep for an hour when Spina returned to the room.

"Scacciato, you silly child!" she cried, her thin face swelled with maternal joy. She wrapped her arms around him, covering him with warmth and the slightly sweaty smell of her hair.

"Come! Your son is born! Your wife and your new son are well and waiting for you."

"What?" He looked wide-eyed at her, tried to understand all at once that he had been asleep but was now awake and also a father. Spina pulled him from the window and walked him toward the door. In the doorway he found his footing and hurried into the room. His two mothers were on the far side of the bed: the old Nurse gray-faced but happy, Cavriuola beaming at no one in particular with her hands clasped as usual in front of her stomach. The mid-wife and a servant stood on the near side of the bed. Emelia, flat on her back, lay still but wonderfully alive and by her side something small and dark moved almost imperceptibly.

Still barely awake and also very much in awe, Scacciato stared at the group, paused briefly at the foot of the bed, then moved to his wife's side, pushing past Cavriuola without a word. He bent over and kissed Emelia - it seemed the thing to do - before looking at the child. It moved, it wiggled, it was clearly alive but it was not yet living to him. It still existed on the other side of a wall in a world of will-be, a world of maybe, a world of yet-to-come.

Cavriuola placed a cool damp hand against her son's cheek. "My Scacciato," she whispered. "Let the sun and the wind tear down the mountains around your heart."

He sometimes made the mistake of thinking, if only briefly, that his mother was sane. He would try to decipher her messages as if they made sense, wasting precious seconds before remembering that she was mad. "Thank you, mother," he said curtly.

He looked down at Emelia and imagined her as a delicate flowering plant ripped apart by a storm but already trying to rebuild, burying new fragile roots into the soil. Her half smile told him that she would be all right; the downward movement of her eyes told him to pick up his son.

Scacciato's hands were pink from the cold. Most of the night he had been rubbing them together constantly but he had forgotten the cold when he entered the bedroom. He was wildly conscious of those hands - wide, long, manly, stiff and pink - as he reached for the child. Even the shadow of his hands covered the infant and made him disappear into the bed covers, as if he could already play hide and seek. Scacciato put one hand behind the child's head and the other under his backside and lifted him gently from the bed. The naked infant was still, quiet, purple and pudgy, with limbs like tiny sausages strung together, skin wet and still smelling of blood, head bulbous and frighteningly soft, separated strands of damp dark hair, glassy blue eyes not focused but moving, trowel-shaped nose awkwardly adult in the middle of the newborn face. His father lifted him closer, stared in awe and fear as the child lay still in his hands for a few seconds, then wiggled his tiny fingers thick as matchsticks and, for the pure hell of it, unleashed a chilling scream that rattled the very walls of the ageless mansion.

Scacciato looked away from the child and fixed his eyes reverently on the far wall, the wall made of thick stone and yet permeated with the winter air. Emelia watched him stare into the stone and thought: He is a proud father. I have made him happy, truly happy for the first time in his life.

As the wailing continued, the old Nurse thought: My baby child now has a baby of his own. I am getting very old but I am still glad for him. He is knowing the feeling of loving a child.

Cavriuola thought: Scacciato can see now what I have tried to show him, that the creatures of the earth are all wonderful and so we must climb the rocks and harvest the plants of our life as we move through the sea, always keeping our eyes and our hearts unblinded to the hopes of the sky.

Spina looked at the man who had scared her minutes before and thought, as the child's murderous screaming got worse: After this he will believe in God and is probably thanking God at this moment for the child.

Scacciato thought: How helpless - just as I was. How easily and rapidly one human can destroy another, especially if the other can be held in a grown man's two hands? Has not someone else thought of the insane power we have over our children?

We need only forget them, leave them unnoticed in a corner and they will starve, put them outside and they will freeze. The power of it, the responsibility, comes equally, to peasants and noblemen the same. Will this little creature spend a lifetime hating me and struggling to overcome my world? If so, I would save him a lot of trouble and pain if I flung him against the stone wall. But perhaps it does not have to be that way. Could it be ...?

Scacciato looked back at the child, who was now quiet but fidgeting, his little fingers blindly picking at his own face, flinching legs reaching out to kick at the air and at the bearded sharp-nosed deep-eyed monster that held him. Scacciato tried to meet eyes with his son but the child only glanced at him for a fraction of a second, allowing no more than the "who the hell are you?" look of an infant to cross his face. Scacciato bent forward until their noses almost touched but again the child darted his eyes to the side as if to find his way around a giant boulder, the extent of which he could not imagine. His father studied him at close range, noted the features that formed the face, all babyish and indistinct except for the nose, a cleaver of identity that spread the face apart and obliterated any chance of anonymity for the child.

When he pulled the infant's hand away from its face, the little fingers - no more than tiny bones with a thin layer of pudge around them - wrapped instinctively and desperately around Scacciato's long first finger, barely able to encircle it. Scacciato held the child even closer, silently commanded him to look his father in the eye, and watched as his son stared at the ceiling. Partly in frustration and partly in whimsy, the father opened his mouth wide and slowly, gently, bit his son on the tip of his nose. He pulled back and looked: for a second or two, not long but just long enough, father and son looked into each others' eyes, something passed, something magic and unknowable moved across generations, something that the son would never remember and the father would never forget. Then it was gone.

"He will have a name!" Scacciato shouted, startling both himself and the women who had watched his exploration of the child with a mixture of reverence and anxiety. With one sentence he ridiculed those who had made his life less tolerable by depriving him of a name except that of Outcast and at the same time carved out of nothingness a major fact of his son's life, for a man's name carries with it a collection of connotations and expectations which he must accept or reject, which can lead him to spend a lifetime trying to live up to the name or a lifetime rebelling against it.

"He will be Giusfredi. Giusfredi is my brother and and now Giusfredi is my son."

Suddenly the temperature in the room dropped as if the winter air had settled down a notch; it almost made a sound like ice settling. As the women frantically tried, each in her own way, to discover the reason that Scacciato would not only reject the name of his father but also his own ghost of a name and turn instead to his brother for a name for the child, Scacciato thought of Giusfredi in the bright yellow outfit he had worn on the wedding day, his brother the simple optimist of action, the spring flower of a man whose name incongruously dominated the dark and chilled bedroom. To speak his name under the conditions of the bitter and bloody February night was to use it out of season, rip it from the warm earth of May by the roots and plunge it into an icy stream on the shadow side of the world where there is no sun, no bright prospering garden of life, no faith and no simplicity, only the complex gloom of eternal light. But there it was: the name Giusfredi flung into the room by his younger brother who was intoxicated with power and authority, oblivious to seasons and climate and man, no longer scared or awkward, in control again.

"Giusfredi is a wonderful name," Emelia whispered, reaching to touch her husband. "Your brother will be very proud."

He smiled at her, pleased that she approved of his choice, not even thinking that he had made it without her. He looked to his right and saw the old Nurse beaming, Cavriuola staring into space with no expression at all, and Spina looking at him with both pride and curiosity on her face. He held the infant in one hand at arm's length in the air and calmly explained: "Giusfredi. Because my brother has never done me any harm."

The child was quiet high in the air but began to wail again during the descent. Scacciato passed him down to Emelia and stepped back, thoughts of revenge, love, anger, and triumph all battling for attention as they rattled through his mind. Here is my world, he thought. Here is the world I create day by day. A child, a wife, and a plan, therein lies completeness. An infant, a woman, and a scheme. This is my life forming before my eyes, gradually taking the shape of my hands, my fingers. The world of my father is retreating into the background. Even this wretched winter belongs to him; the springtime will be mine.

"You must let them get some rest," Spina said, easing between Scacciato and Cavriuola. "Let us go down and celebrate with some food and drink. Perhaps Capece will come and Giusfredi should be home soon."

"Please tell my father," Emelia said softly. "I know you do not like to speak to him and you will probably have to wake him up. But I want him to know tonight that our son has been born."

He nodded; at that moment nothing bothered him, not even speaking to the disgusting d'Oria. Emelia thanked him with her eyes and a squeeze of the hand that he gave to her. Leaving the servants to look after the new mother and child, Scacciato hurried through the sitting room and into the corridor with Cavriuola, Spina, and the Nurse following him. They began to laugh and intertwined their arms like a family on holiday. He managed to accept the feeling of family that dominated the scene even though his mind was on his father's destruction as much as it was on little Giusfredi's arrival.

As they made their way down the front stairs, alternating between lackadaisical strolling and playful marching, he thought how odd the juxtaposition of feelings was, his simultaneous appreciation of both creation and destruction. He could not focus on both notions for long because as they reached the landing at the second floor, they heard the commotion of horses outside and the rushing of servants inside, signaling the arrival of one of the members of the household. From the volume of the racket, Scacciato assumed it was Capece, who usually brought home several of his cronies when he visited the mansion instead of staying in town. Giusfredi always rode home alone.

"There is someone now," Spina said, ebullient with anticipation. "Perhaps it is Capece or maybe Giusfredi." She spoke as if it did not matter which man it was but Scacciato did not notice. He put his arm around her waist and proceeded down the stairs with Cavriuola immediately behind them and the Nurse following as fast as she could.

They reached the first floor landing just as Capece and three of his friends - all old, overweight, and loud - came through the front door which they left flung open. Scacciato barely had time to focus his loathing before the drunk d'Oria appeared in the banquet hall doorway supported by two servant boys about the age Scacciato was when he had been freed. Waves of bitter air rushed into the house as servants - women and young boys - raced down the entrance hall to take the heavy coats, scarves, and caps.

Scacciato paused on the landing while the women swirled past him. He stopped thinking for only a few seconds, then realized that here on the night of his joy and scheming optimism, he was still not the master of his life, his moods, his emotions. His center was outside of himself; his center was a beam of sinister light aimed first at Capece and then at d'Oria. He wanted to desroy them both.

He fell against the wall and watched in horror as the scene unfolded below. Capece berated the frightened servants for not bringing them drink even though their arms were still loaded up with coats and scarves. The servants scurried away to replace the warmth of clothing with the warmth of wine. One had the presence of mind to shut the door.

The men stepped further into the foyer; Capece looked expectantly at the women in front of him. Spina rushed to meet him with the news. Scacciato warched Spina and Capece embrace, then saw the old Nurse stand to the side, shyly ignoring the rough talk of Capece's companions. Cavriuola stood nearby with hands folded a few inches in front of her stomach, head straight up and still but ready to twitch to the side if danger came, one foot lifted at the heel, prepared for motion, the way a horse or a mule stands at rest.

At the same time, he heard the sound of another horse outside, a solitary rider in the night, one without companions and probably without wine, one with only his clothes and his soul to provide him with protection against the cold: his brother Giusfredi, home from his council duties late in the evening as always. The thought of his brother gave him hope. After all, this was the night of Scacciato and Giusfredi, Scacciato the father and not the son, Giusfredi the brother and Giusfredi the son. It was not the night of silly women tittering about, giddy from their proximity to another woman giving birth, not the night of rattling old men smelling of leather and drink and horses. He would go to the door and greet his brother with the news, with the wondrous present only Scacciato could give him, and for a few moments they would be close again. They could share the innocence and whimsy of childhood that they had experienced so rarely when they were young and never after they were grown.

He spread his right hand out against the wall and pushed himself into motion, all but falling down the few steps beneath the landing, stalked past the women, hoped against all reason that he could walk unacknowledged past Capece. The moment came loose in time for Scacciato; it seemed to last forever and race like a lunatic's raving at the same time. Like three slaps in the face, three sounds cracked through the frosted air and staggered Scacciato's composure.

The first: "My son, you have a son!" Capece shouted. The second: "Ah, my boy!" d'Oria bellowed. The third: the storm-beaten door smashed open. Scacciato jumped past Capece who stood with his arms squeezing the smiling voluptuous Spina, ignored d'Oria's drunken shouts from across the room, and looked toward his brother standing in the entrance-way with the storm as a backdrop.

The noises blurred together: laughter of women, hoarse barking of drunken old men, howling of wind, heaving splattering of raindrops at Giusfredi's feet. He stood and watched as a look appeared on his brother's face which he had never seen there before, a hard and cruel look. He spun around and saw the grinning old bear Capece with one arm still around Spina and one around Cavriuola, who tolerated it as a cat allows a human to rub its fur.

Having read the emotion in his brother's face, Scacciato stepped backward, suddenly finding himself unable to speak. He turned away, closed his eyes, and said to himself: I will make a world where my son will not have to hate me.

VI

About the time little Giusfredi took his first steps, Scacciato's scheme to topple Arrighetto had begun to take shape. Shortly after Emelia gave birth, Scacciato convinced Capece to turn over the managment of the family's finances to him. The argument itself was simple: the estate and its farming generated a huge amount of money but nothing was done with it because there was no one who spent the time it took to invest and expand the wealth. Capece could not be a financial manager and also handle the affairs of state. Giusfredi, although he was the oldest son, was not shrewd enough to do it. Scacciato, on the other hand, had the intelligence, the learning, the mathematical skills, the languages that would be helpful in foreign ventures, and the practical experience of running the estate. Furthermore, he had streamlined the operations in Sicily such that he had more than enough time to pursue investments abroad. He argued that he could build the small Capece empire into one of the most powerful fortunes in the Mediterranean.

Capece was intrigued but sent Scacciato away so that he could consider the plan. When he called his son into town a few days later and sat across from him in his spacious governor's chambers, he had only one question.

"Will all this investment, this speculation, will it in any way limit my access to whatever funds I might need?"

"There will be a fund of gold coins in the vault of the mansion for you and only you, father."

They shook hands and parted, the old man sure that he was destined to be richer than his wildest dreams thanks to this moody but brilliant son who was finally coming around, the son sure that he would some day see his father in tears at his feet.

From then through the end of the summer, Scacciato pursued the most obvious and profitable of investments. The family fortune went into shipping and commodities and, since he devoted virtually all of his time to it, Scacciato quickly turned profits. He purchased a ship on the mainland and filled it with goods that he knew the aristocracy in Sicily would buy, then sold the stuff as a lot to a broker at a huge profit. Afterwards he refilled the ship with whatever crops he could buy and sailed back to the mainland to sell the load for another profit. By repeating the process several times, he not only improved the standard of living for the Sicilians but also bought a ship each time he crossed the water, acquiring a small fleet within a matter of months. These he sold to a Genoan firm. He hired an assistant to start the process over again, this time purchasing five ships instead of one, and set off across Italy with the rest of the money, looking for more avenues of profit.

Profit he found but, more importantly for his purposes, he became well-known throughout Italy as a shrewd and driven man, one who could cut a deal with nobility or with known scoundrels if it would make him money. He learned that there were good reasons to work not only with aristocrats but also with those of less savory reputation. One scoundrel leads to another and that one to another. A man can construct a stiff chain of questionable contacts such that he is in a position to wiggle one end of the chain to make the other move and the one end does not know and cannnot find out who did the wiggling. Thus he began to create for himself a web of intermediaries which allowed him to channel the family gold wherever he wished, and neither the family nor the ultimate recipient of the money knew what he was doing and would not know until Scacciato was ready.

It was in this concatented way that Scacciato began to loan money to the Pope. In moderate sums at first, then larger and larger, he passed money to one agent with instructions to take a healthy commission and pass it on to another agent and then another along with a password (he chose the word "bist"). Far down the line, some agent who did not know Scacciato or Capece or even that the money was Sicilian would receive instructions from the unseen "Bist," delivered by yet another agent, well-paid but not part of the original chain, to contact a representative of the Vatican treasury that Scacciato had discovered was charged with the enormous fund-raising required to keep the Pope and his armies supplied with what they needed. The agent would turn over the cash in exchange for papal bonds and pass them back down the line.

The man in the middle of the chain, however, was part of two chains. He received money from one man but when the bonds came back down, he gave them to a third agent unknown to any of the rest. This agent passed the bonds along through three other men, all anti-papal fanatics who believed that they were a part of a plot to ruin the Pope at some future date by demanding payment for the bonds at some inopportune time. The last one knew Scacciato only as "Doe-child" and met him in a dark seaside tavern to turn over the bonds and receive his generous payment from the young man who never looked out from under the brim of his hat.

Scacciato kept his promise to his father; he made sure that Capece's fund was maintained. He also kept a secret fund for himself hidden behind a loose brick in the wall of his bedroom. He diverted enough money to keep the entire household not simply comfortable but prosperous. On his visits home from Italy, he was the darling of the family. He accepted their praise and love and he smiled a lot.

Then events beyond his control forced Scaccciato to accelerate his plans. King James succeeded to the throne of Aragon and left his rule of Sicily to his younger brother Frederick. For several months, Capece ruled the island by himself while waiting for the young Spaniard to make his desultory way to Sicily to claim his throne. Scacciato never had the patience to keept straight the details of Sicilian politics. All he cared about and knew for certain was that Capece was always on the opposite side from the Pope.

He feared that the change from King James to King Frederick might somehow complicate his plans. He also worried that the papal forces would mount some offensive against Sicily while the transition from one king to another was in process. He began to funnel money into papal bonds at a breathtaking rate, selling off ships and storehouses of goods at a minimal profit if it brought more gold under his control right away. He in effect liquidated the family fortune and converted it into a bulging leather bag full of papal bonds.

The bag slapped against his side as he walked down the hall with one hand grasping the shoulder strap and the other hand swinging in the air like a schoolboy's. He started to whistle but stopped himself and assumed a more serious expression. He hoped that Capece was in the bedroom so that he would not have to chase around the mansion for him. Cavriuola was out for a carriage ride (she often took them when Capece was home), Emelia was with little Giusfredi in the garden, and his brother and Spina were downstairs. Giusfredi had taken the day off from his council duties and had requested a family dinner since they all were at home at the same time for a change. He still tried to make them a family at the slightest opportunity. But the fact that they were all occupied and that no one had seen d'Oria for days - he was probably off on one of his binges - meant that he and the old man would be alone and no one would be likely to intrude on them.

Scacciato had aged much during his year and a half of wily maneuvering. He had spent a lot of time outdoors in his travels, much of it at sea, and his face was dark and weathered. He often ate pooorly and drank too much wine on his excursions, although he always exercised before bedtime to retain his strength. He was still healthy but he looked older than his twenty-four years. He had taken the habit of wearing rough sailor's clothing - he never cared for fashion - and that made him look older as well. But the lines around his eyes and across his forehead were not from the weather, his diet, or his clothes. They were from scheming, his lying awake at night on strange ships and in foreign rooming houses, lying awake and plotting, calculating.

He had not been in his parents' chambers for years. His hand trembled as he knocked. A servant girl opened the door and looked relieved when he asked her to leave him alone with his father. He did not notice the outer rooms he walked through, in fact did not seem to have vision at all until his eyes found Arrighetto Capece sprawled on the bed in his unbuttoned riding clothes, evidently preparing to leave.

The old man had always been big but now he was fat. He bulged in his clothes and the meat hung dryly from his neck. His beard was grey and his matted hair scraggly and thinning. The fire of battle was still in his eyes but there was a hollowness around them that contrasted with the puffy well-fed skin of his sagging face. Age and circumstances were catching up with warrior, as if his body had held together through the hard times only to collapse in flaccid decay during the recent years of luxury and overindulgence. He was drinking already and there was a tray of food remnants beside him on the bed. The bed, constructed by a local tradesman specifically for Capece, was huge: eight feet wide and four feet off the floor. Silk coverings and thick spreads were in disarray, as were a half dozen fat fringed pillows.

"Come in, my son," he shouted. He took a drink of wine but did not offer any to his son. "How is the family fortune today?" He followed this with a long laugh as he pulled himself up and leaned on one elbow.

"I've got it under control," Scacciato said, gripping the bag under his arm.

"Then what brings you here?"

"I have come here to explain to you your impending destruction."

Capece sat up, grunted, laughed half a laugh but sucked it in, grunted again. He knew his son was serious. The look in Scacciato's eyes disturbed him. He also remembered that his fortune had been in Scacciato's hands for over a year. As his heart sank, he raised his eyebrows as if that could pull it back up, as if he could change what his heart did by will, as if he could change what had already happened. "Yes?" he asked simply.

"There is enough of your fortune left for the rest of the family, in a place you will never find. But the rest is invested in your downfall, your political ruin. It is all in papal bonds, notes from the Pope. Your fortune has for months been financing the Pope's armies."

"The Pope," he said. "The Pope." His eyes rolled back and forth a few times, then looked straight ahead. "You did this?" There was a touch of respect in his voice.

"Yes. And soon I will make this public. Arrighetto Capece, who has made a career of fighting the Papacy, financing the Pope's armies. Betraying your country for the huge interest payments, the easy profits. It should make quite a scandal. Perhaps you will be hung or perhaps thrown back into prison or perhaps simply exiled. I don't care. Although I would love to see them parade you through the streets, bound and slung over the back of an ass. But ..." He waved his arms and understood that he really did not care about the details of Capece's punishment. "All that matters is that you are ruined."

"And you? What will they do to you?"

"Nothing. I will explain that I was acting on my father's orders, sworn to secrecy, but that my love for Sicily overcame my loyalty to my father so I had to expose you. They will do nothing to me. I may even become a hero." He stood as still as his mother, calm and self-contained for the most important moment of his life.

Capece stared at his son for a moment, expressionless, then lay back down on the bed with his face turned away. Scacciato watched him, savoring the moment, thinking to himself that the sight of Capece motionless and quiet and defeated was the most beautiful sight he had ever seen, even more wonderful than he had dreamed it would be. He realized that what he felt - more than joy or triumph or power - was relief, relief that the battle was over and that now his life could begin.

He saw Capece's torso shudder slightly. He thought he heard a muffled sound. Was the old man crying? There it was again, harder and louder. What strange manner of tears are these? he thought. Tears? This is laughter! Has the old man gone mad?

Capece swung himself up and let his feet fall to the floor, holding himself up with his hands, arms stiffened, and laughed like mad thunder. Tears came but they fell into a mouth twisted with hilarity. He sucked a deep watery breath and laughed again for a minute, finally settling into a smile with which he obliterated his son's composure.

"A good try, my son," he chuckled. "A very good try. I congratulate you on your skill and cunning. And your hatred. A good man must know how to hate well." He paused, wiped the tears of laughter from his eyes, and looked again at his son, who stood in the same position as before but with a face more confused than it had ever been. "But it is too late, my little schemer. You see, I am already ruined. I could not tell anyone because some turncoat would try to have my hide or there would be panic among the locals. But you see this younger brother of King James, this Frederick who is on his way to become king, he detests me. Some silly matter about his wife, once when I went to Spain on state business. It was nothing, really, an afternoon dalliance." He made a face, laughed, and continued.

"But he hates me like a weed, you see. Has just yesterday sent me a notice by messenger to get the hell out of Sicily. Says he will confiscate my estate and have me hanged if he finds me here. He is on his way to the island right now. I hear his party should be here within a week. So I must be gone. Papal bonds ..." He laughed again, fell back on the bed, then pulled himself back up and talked on through the laughter. "...or no papal bonds!" He fell back again, throwing his arms up into the air, and continued to chuckle.

Again! Scacciato thought. Again my fate is snatched out of my hands by strangers! I would have freed myself from slavery if given a little time but events and political vicissitudes and people I barely knew preempted my actions! Now my dreams of destroying this beast are shattered because some stranger, some nonentity of a Spaniard has already decreed his destruction! What in the hell is going on here?

He staggered backward, dazed and deafened by Capece's mocking laughter. He reached out behind him and found the arm of a heavily-padded chair and collapsed into it. Across the room, Capece sat up on the edge of the bed. Scacciato fell into a vertiginous orgy of self-pity and buried himself in the utter disaster of the moment, of his life, of the wreckage of his grand plan. He was not sure at first that Capece was making words again.

"Yes, a good try, my boy, a very good try. But I cannot linger and congratulate you, celebrate your near triumph with a few drinks." Scacciato pulled himself to the edge of the chair, desperate and out of control, paying attention without knowing why. "My loyal comrades," Capece continued. "Yes, both of them - ha! - are coming for me at nightfall. We will flee in the darkness and deprive the Spaniard of his pleasure of executing me. Yes, I will get away. Of course I will get away. I always do. But now ..." He sat up on the side of the bed. "Now I will go find an errand for your brother to run and while he is gone I will - for one last delicious time - spike his lovely wife Spina."

Scacciato stiffened and blurted out the word: "What?"

"Spina," he said casually, as he smoothed his clothes with his hands. "I will go ... What?" He looked incredulously at his second son. "You didn't know? Ha!" He bellowed that immoral laugh again, then stopped to look at Scacciato. "You really did not know? Perhaps you are not so smart after all. The whole mansion, I am sure, hell, half the town probably knows I have been bedding your brother's wife for years."

The voice inside said: It is time. He never remembered his feet touching the floor or crossing the room though they surely did. The hands, the preternaturally murderous hands, wrapped around scaly neckflesh, not Little Vision's, not d'Oria's, but Capece's at last. Two decades of hatred, five years of training, a year of vengeful obsession, and a moment's worth of utter disgust rushed like crazed blood into those hands that became a part of Capece's neck as a heavy vine becomes a part of the tree that it is destroying.

The old man was not without some of his old strength. After an instant of shock when his son first landed on him and pinned him to the bed, Capece grasped Scacciato's hands and tried to pull them away. There was power still in his arms and for a few moments he believed that he would fling this mad child to the floor and walk in pride to Spina's chambers. He slipped his fingers around Scacciato's wrists, trying to pull the hands away and at the same time squeezing the vessels on the under-side of the wrists to weaken the grip.

Then his mind went blank, not entirely comprehending that he could not tear his son's hands away and could not even weaken the grasp that was beginning to stop the flow of air into his lungs. But it was not this failure that made him panic. It was the look, not of madness, but of rational and calculating mechanical hatred in his son's eyes. Scacciato stared down over his hawk nose, watching Capece as a man watches a chicken when he rings its neck before dinnner. Capece fought with his legs and lower trunk, flailed upward against Scacciato's lean frame, hoping to shake him loose from down below since he could not break free of those hands like the jaws of a monster around his neck.

A strength he never dreamed his son could have met him; Scacciato dug his knees up into Capece's rib cage and the pain not only took away most of what was left of his strength but also took away his will to fight. He instinctively kept his fingers curled around Scacciato's fingertips, al-most unconsciously using the remnants of his strength to attempt to pry even one finger loose. But it was only instinct, a self-preservation urge lodged in the psyche of the animal to fight to the end, if only feebly. A milky film came over his vision, Scacciato's face blurred, faded, and it was over.

Scacciato squeezed the fleshy neck long after the surprise, the dis-belief, the fear, and finally the resignation had passed from the old man's eyes, after they had become distant and ghostly clear. It was only after he realized that there had been no breathing for a long time, that the massive chest no longer heaved but lay flat and still, that he slowly released his hands, then cautiously backed his way off the bed. The first thing he felt as he stood up, trembling from the fight, was the pain in his hands. He looked down at them, felt them burning, saw that they were still cupped.

He looked at the doorway as if to be sure there was an exit from this chamber of death. He picked up the leather bag, full of the papal bonds, now useless to him, and began to walk through his father's chambers, halting at the doorway. "It is over," he muttered aloud. "It's really over. . .But, damn it, the bastard made me kill him. Now I will be hung."

He forced himself into the corridor, but had not gone far when he heard a racket on the far stairwell. He knew it was Giusfredi but he kept to his route and soon stood face to face with his brother.

"Scacciato," he said cautiously, in the way he always greeted his brother.

Scacciato looked at Giusfredi with the eyes of a madman. He was too numb to speak at first, but then he said, "You had better go to our father's rooms. I seem to have killed him."

"My brother," he said quietly. "Why?"

Scacciato did not hesitate or weigh his words; he simply answered honestly. "Because he's been sporting with your wife. For years, I suppose." He understood from the look on his brother's face that Giusfredi had suspected but had not known. He had never been told by anyone whose words he could not dismiss as vicious gossip, had not been told by anyone who had no reason to lie to him. Scacciato realized at the same time that he had, in ten minutes, taken away his brother's father and also the one thing that gave Giusfredi reason to continue his life: his delusion that he was not being betrayed.

Unwilling to watch his brother's face crumbling under the tears, he continued walking, went down the two flights of stairs outside, and walked for no reason to the stables. Once inside in the dark with the smell of animals, leather, and hay all around, he knew that he needed a few minutes alone before someone, whoever it would be, came to arrest him and ask him dozens of questions. He hid the leather bag in a box of rags - though he did not know why he bothered - and walked to the back of the stable. There he found an empty stall and sat down on a pile of hay-sprinkled blankets in the dark corner. The instant he sat down he found something soft and flabby beneath him. When the pile of blankets groaned, he leaped across the stall and watched in disgust as d'Oria, smelling of wine and vomit, rolled out from underneath them. He faced Scacciato but never opened his eyes and continued with his drunken sleep.

Prison, Scacciato said to himself. The only place I can be alone and find some peace is in prison. I might as well get it over with. He left the stable, crossed the gardens, and found a smoothed spot in the grass in front of the mansion. There he stretched out, propped his elbow on the ground, and leaned his head against his hand, waiting to be taken away.

VII

He waited a long time on the lawn of the mansion. No one would go near him, not the family, not the servants. After almost an hour, Cavriuola came out and stood in front of the door, looking in all directions except Scacciato's. He watched her stand there still except for the rotating of her head and the fluttering of her long thin dress. Finally she locked eyes with him. He stared back, a slight smile appeared on her face, and she went back inside. Later someone finally had the presence of mind to send to town for some of Capece's assistants to come and investigate. When they finally came, three somber men on horseback, he calmly told them: "I killed him."

Two stayed with him (several feet away) while the other, a giant of a man named Alfonse, went inside to ask about details. Scacciato knew Alfonse slightly, had always tolerated him more than any of Capece's cronies, found him quieter and more spiritual in some way than the others, and was glad that Alfonse had come for him. What he did not know was that the reserved and introspective Alfonse had hated the bawdy boisterous Capece and had endured him only because he paid him well to tower behind him during any moment of confrontation or tension, and that Alfonse had heard the news of the murder without surprise and with some amusement. So Alfonse took it on himself to go to the mansion and conduct the inquiry and arrest in person. It was because of this that his statements to Scacciato on the lawn were simple, gently spoken, and almost apologetic, even though Alfonse would soon take him to the prison and personally close the thick wooden door and turn the key.

The prison was in the center of town, a four-story building near one corner of the square, convenient for hangings. The front faced the square and the other three sides overlooked narrow dark alleys that separated them from the adjacent buildings. As they rode up to the prison, Scacciato unbound on the back of Alfonse's horse, they felt an air of anarchy and confusion in the town. There was nothing specific, only a sense of too much activity, too much nervous laughter, and perhaps an insouciant air about the tradesmen and loafers who watched them ride across the square. Inside, there was much muffled important talk which resulted in a lower-level official of the council charging Scacciato with murder and ordering him to remain incarcerated until such time as the town council scheduled a hearing or a trial or something.

Alfonse led him up a nearly black musty stairwell that smelled of urine and mold. At the top floor (a position given to Scacciato in deference to his background because the fourth floor was considered less oppressive), Alfonse opened an iron windowless door with one of the many keys he carried on his belt and motioned Scacciato in. A long corridor stretched before him, dark but with a slight glow from the sunlight that fell into the outer cells and was then refracted through the tightly barred one foot square window in each cell door. At last Alphone stopped - Scacciato almost walked into him - and opened a cell door. As it swung open, light from the outside window flooded into the hallway and someone in a cell nearby groaned. Scacciato breathed deeply and walked into the room, ten feet by less than six feet wide, furnished with a stone bench, an urn reeking of defecation, and on the floor a wooden basin dry but warped from years of holding water.

He stood looking at the window, the last remnant of his connection with the world. He barely heard Alfonse say "I will have some water brought up," and said nothing when the door slammed and the key screeched in the lock. He mechanically stepped to the bench and sat with his back against the cool stones. He relaxed, enjoyed the vacant feeling in his mind, and put the back of his head against the wall. As it touched, he felt a delicious chill run down his neck and spread across his shoulders, then through his spine. He laughed, stopped, then laughed again and again, as Capece had laughed before his death.

Alfonse returned to the cell, looked in at the young prisoner, and reopened the door. Scacciato turned and through his tears saw Alfonse for the first time. Suddenly people were no longer either members of his family or strangers but individuals with characteristics of their own. The man was more than six and a half feet tall, and seemed as wide as Little Vision was tall. A boyish face with small dark eyes squinted out from under the brim of his hat.

"Scacciato, are you all right?" he asked in an almost motherly tone.

He laughed and slapped his knees. "I am sitting in a tiny prison cell and I've just begun to wait for my probable execution. Of course I'm all right!" He slapped his knees again and bounced his feet on the floor, giggling like a schooboy with a secret. He waved for the puzzled man to join him. "Come here, Alfonse. Sit here and let me explain."

Alfonse left the door open - he knew there was no danger of the young man half his size escaping - and sat beside Scacciato on the bench. This is certainly strange, he thought. Either the maddest or the sanest creature I ever met.

"It is only this, my friend." He put his hand on Alfonse's leg, ready to reach out to a member of the human race, a brotherhood he had never felt he belonged to before, one which had been irrelevant for his purposes. Humanity interested him in a new, personal sense now that the anger that had defined his short tortured life had evaporated with the sweat from his hands around Capece's neck.

"I always liked you, Alfonse, though I never knew you, only noticed you as one of my father's people who did not have his stench. May I confide in you?"

"Speak," Alfonse replied.

"I want you to know, my friend, that I feel sad for Emelia and my son. But they are young, they will recover and endure. And I believe that I have passed to them a freedom which they would never have known otherwise, a freedom which will be consummated when my feet swing in the town square.

"You see, I have never known freedom before. Yes, I was freed from d'Oria's kitchen and lived in the mansion and travelled and made a fortune. Yet I was never free *inside* before. Am I making sense?"

"Yes, I think so."

"Well, even though I am in this disgusting cell waiting to die, I at last have taken an action that was all mine and world-shaking, and because what little time I have left is all mine. Since they will kill me anyway, there is nothing left that anyone can do to me. Do you understand that I am the freest person in Sicily at this moment? Do you see why I laugh and feel like a child, an innocent and unshackled child for the first time in my life?"

Alfonse looked down at Scacciato and felt something akin to caring and a respect he had not felt for a long time. He had had a wife once that he felt that for but she had tired of the long absences required by his profession as a soldier and had simply disappeared years before. With no family, only a few friends he drank with, and a life which until a few hours before revolved around a man he could not stand, he had felt those emotions only as memories until this moment. It occurred to him also that Scacciato had set him free just as much as he had freed himself. He put one big hand on Scacciato's shoulder.

"I cannot help you much. I cannot let you escape or save your life. But I will try to make it as easy as I can for you. Because, just between you and me, your father was a pig. I'm glad he's gone too."

"Ha!" he said, slapping the big man on the leg. "I just knew you were sane."

They laughed together, the laugh of men freed from ceremony and position, the laugh of comrades, of brothers. Slowly a melancholy descended on Alfonse as he thought of his new friend with a broken neck and rope burns. He desperately wished that he could extricate Scacciato somehow but he knew that he could not. He squeezed the young man on the shoulder and left without a word.

Three days passed during which Scacciato's only visitor was Alfonse. The giant brought him water frequently and sneaked him better food than the other prisoners received. The reason he was allowed no visitors was that the town council was in a state of disarray. With the governor dead and the new king still en route to the capital, no one knew exactly who should make decisions, even small ones such as whether or not Scacciato should have visitors. They were not even sure if there was a requirement that a trial be held or if they should simply go ahead and hang him since he had confessed to the murder.

For three days he sat in his cell, sleeping very little, feeling like a creature freed from all but the most minimal physical needs. He ate distractedly and not much, he sipped on the water that Alfonse insisted he should drink, and he catnapped, but most of the time he lay on the stone bench and stared at the window, at the sunlight or the darkness on the other side. He stared not longingly, as if his need was to reach that openness beyond the bars. He stared at it in a contented spiritual way, believing that what was out there, what most men dreamed of or fought for, was already in his heart. He felt a connection to the light and darkness and a sense of freedom that had nothing to do with physical bonds, nothing to do with situation or circumstance, only with spirit and mind. He rarely even walked to the window to look out; he knew what the wall of the other building looked like because he had looked at it once and that was enough. He thought often of Emelia and little Giusfredi, daydreamed about the kind of life they might have after he was gone, believed sincerely as he had told Alfonse that they would be all right, that life would be kind to them. He waited for his death and never, not once, did he ever consider that he might yet go free.

On the morning of the fourth day, the key turned in the lock. He did not bother to raise himself from the bench or move his eyes from the square of light. He assumed it was Alfonse with some breakfast, perhaps biscuits again. But he immediately smelled something different. For three days he had smelled nothing but the fetid stone of his cell and the emissions of his own body, interrupted two or three times a day by the dusty, leathery smell of Alfonse and the dull aromas of the bland food. With no other smells for that long a time, he instantly sensed the presence of something else at the door of the cell without seeing or hearing anything different. It was a scent he knew well, it was the smell of a human, it was a smell of cleanness and sweetness and soft satin, ruffles, and lace. It was Emelia.

He swung up and around in one movement, leaped to her in the doorway and held her as if for the first time, gently but with a feeling of connection untarnished by anger. She squeezed him much harder, returning his light touch of undistracted love with a desperate and terrified grasp. He breathed her in, smelled her hair as if it was his first breath, felt her tears against his skin without sadness, only acceptance. He knew that the moment could not be the same for her as for him, that she could not feel the peace he knew. For her, life had taken a strange and ominous turn, leaving her on her own in a state of uncertainty. Neither of them noticed that Alphonse remained at the doorway, unobtrusive but necessary. Scacciato drew Emelia to his bench and they sat down, arms still around each other, her face buried in his neck. It was several minutes before she lifted her head and looked at him.

"My poor Scacciato," she said. "My love, what will become of you?

He held back his honesty and tried to change the subject. "I am well. I am eating well and getting lots of rest. I feel better than I have in years. What about you? And little Giusfredi? Are you taking care of yourself?"

She shook her head. "Oh Scacciato, forget about us. Aren't you going mad in here? And for what are you being punished? Because that old bear is dead? Who cares? I don't even believe you did it. I refuse to believe that you did it." She spoke feverishly, trying to convince him of what she truly believed, that he did not strangle his father to death. "I know you are taking the blame for someone else. I just feel it inside me. And other people think so too. We know you hated him, but murder was not your way. You would have destroyed him some other way, using your intelligence, not your hands. The crime does not speak of you."

"Oh, Emelia," was all he could say as he stroked her hair.

"And after all of this, my poor darling," she said, touching his face. "After all of this I must bring you more bad news. I must tell you of even more tragedy in the family."

He was stunned. He believed that tragedy had ended when Capece stopped breathing, that there was nothing else of significance to happen during the remainder of his lifetime. He could only look at her.

"Your brother, Giusfredi, he has hanged himself. He is dead."

"What?" He had overlooked how deeply Giusfredi might have been touched by all that had happened, even though he had played a significant if passive role in the entire chain of events.

"Last night Spina found him in their chambers, hanging from a beam by a rope with a chair beneath him. That is why the council has allowed me to come to you, to bring you the news of your brother's death."

"Giusfredi killed himself? But why?"

Emelia was puzzled by the question but attempted an answer anyway. "No one ... well ... no one exactly ... well he didn't say or leave a letter or anything. In fact he said nothing. He had not uttered a word since he found your father. He only brought Spina to show her the body, took her by the arm and silently led her there, then walked out into the garden. We all tried to talk to him but he would only stare at us and not say anything."

He was saddened by the picture of his brother sitting speechless in the garden and then still not uttering a word for three days before hanging himself.

"He did not say anything?"

"No. Not one single word to anyone."

"Did he ever leave the mansion?"

"No. He never left the grounds. He slept under a blanket out in the garden, sat on a bench all day."

He paused, the world shifting in his mind, the planets and the stars suddenly become unhinged, gravity turning upside down, black becoming white, night become day, madness and sanity fused, wild calculation reeling through his spirit. Through a tiny crack in the stone prison wall spilled light from millions of miles away. "He did not say a word?"

"No, Scacciato." She was a little annoyed at his persistence on that one point. "He never said a word. And now he is dead. He will never say another word."

"My dear, a moment ago you said you believed that I was covering up for someone."

"Some people think you killed Capece, the authorities and the simple townspeople. What else can they think when you told them you did on the lawn, when you willingly came to prison? They have no choice but to accept your word since there were no witnesses. But I will never believe it."

Scacciato tried very hard not to smile. How beautifully his mind worked! how instantly it sorted out the possibilities, listed the points of evidence and quickly concluded that there was one simple path to choose. He also wanted to smile, perhaps even laugh, because his brother, by remaining mute for the last three days of his life, had left him a present, a wonderful present. He could not let the smile emerge, however. He had to remain serious and become, for a few minutes, the greatest actor the world had ever seen.

"My Emelia." He looked down, then into her eyes. He touched her face, ran his fingers across her nose. "I cannot go on like this.

Tragedy sweeps through our family like the wind. But I cannot go on, not with my brother dead. I believed that he would take care of you all and you would not need me, but now..." He paused for effect.

"Yes?"

"I have to confess now. Yes, I was protecting someone." He spoke slightly louder so that Alfonse, leaning forward in the doorway without embarrassment, could hear every word. "I did not kill my father. I found him, yes, with the murderer standing over him. I took the blame to protect that person. But I cannot continue, not when my family has no head."

"Who?" she begged, wanting to hear and not wanting to hear at the same time. "Who killed Capece? Who killed him?"

He looked down again. His face hardened with sadness but inside his heart was filled with satisfaction as he conjured up the picture of Guasparrino d'Oria swinging on the scaffold in the square, his bugged-out eyes straining against the force of the rope, Scacciato's rope.

"Your father, my dear. Guasparrino d'Oria murdered Capece."

It was not as bad as he thought it would be. A tear formed in each eye. She looked away, but then smiled back at him. "I am not surprised. I always knew my father would come to a bad end. Everyone knows they hated each other. They even fought on our wedding day." She sniffled. "I remember my father wrestling in the dust with your father." Scacciato remembered d'Oria drunk and asleep, without alibi, probably without recolleciton of the previous few days, under the straw and blankets in the barn. He almost laughed. "But I am not his daughter any more. I am your wife. And I stand with you. You are the most noble man in the world. You tried to spare me this grief over my father by taking the blame for him, a man you despised. You are an incredible man, Scacciato."

Alfonse could longer pretend he was not listening. He stepped forward into the cell. "Scacciato? What you say...It was d'Oria who killed the old bast- ...pardon me, my lady, who killed old Capece? You have been taking the blame for him?" His eyes were full of hope, glad that he might yet be able to unlock the prison door for his young friend, relieved that Capece was dead and no one of any good would have to pay for it.

"It is true, my friend. I cannot protect the man now when my family needs me. There is Emelia and our son, there is Spina and her children, there is. . .there is my mother," he said, as if the last of his burdens was too obvious to mention.

Alfonse all but leaped into the air with excitement. "I will go to the council at once! I will explain it all to them! You will be free by noon. I am so glad for you Scacciato and sad for you, my lady, but of course these things happen." He did not care how his words sounded though he did not want to offend her. He decided to stop talking and ran from the room.

It took less than an hour for Alfonse to explain the details to the council, still in session waiting for Emelia to finish her visit, and for them to conclude that there was no legal or political reason that they should not set Scacciato free immediately and send a squad to find d'Oria and replace him in Scacciato's cell. During the hour, Scacciato and Emelia sat quietly together, holding one another and savoring the touches after their days of separation. Scacciato leaned his head against the wall and ran his hand up and down Emelia's back, thinking.

What is this all about? A few minutes ago I was at peace, content to face my death simply because I had rid the planet of that wretched Capece, never giving a thought to old d'Oria. And now the rope that was meant for me will be for him and he will die for the crime I gladly committed. Hmmm. Does this twist of fate make a clean sweep of the past?

My life is certainly more important than d'Oria's. He is old, he is scum, he is nothing. He will never do anything of substance. I may yet change the world and he will only drink until he dies. His only creditable act was fathering this young woman and she is good despite his blood, not because of it. Anyone would have done what I did, I suppose. Or perhaps not.

The next two days were the most miraculous of his life. d'Oria had no alibi and they found a leather bag of bonds belonging to Capece in the old drunk's room. After d'Oria's arrest, Scacciato appeared before the council and accepted their apologies for any inconveniences he might have experienced. They asked him to return the following morning to discuss certain matters of state left unfinished by the governor. Scacciato agreed and walked out into the daylight with Emelia and Alfonse on either side. They rode through the town square toward home, acknowledging an occasional cheer from a peasant or a merchant as they passed. At the mansion, he sent Emelia in before him to explain to the other women the events of the morning. He stood with Alfonse on the front lawn, at the very spot where he had been arrested.

"What will you do now, Scacciato?"

"I'm not sure, Alfonse. There is still a lot of wealth buried in these walls." Scacciato glanced away, wondering if someone would make a connection between him and the papal bonds. Could he explain that away as well? He put it out of his mind.

"No one knows what will happen when the new king arrives. He had ordered Capece to be killed, you know. It is hard to say how he will react to your family's continued presence here. What a damned stewpot our lovely Sicily is."

"You're right. Only a few hours ago I was waiting to die. Who knows the future?" Their conversation had nowhere else to go so they waited for Emelia and watched the sky, two men sure of little beyond their new friendship which Scacciato cemented by slipping Alphonse a small bag of gold coins.

The family welcomed Scacciato back with tears and embraces. Spina seemed to be relieved to have someone of strength in the house again beside herself but she said very little. Cavriuola almost seemed to understand what had transpired although all she said was "It is a long path across the sea" when she welcomed him into her arms. The children, the infant Giusfredi and all of Spina's, were delighted to have the dark-eyed young man back with them. He held his son in his arms and walked through the mansion with Spina's brood circling him. He was a symbol of happiness in a household lately filled with sadness; it was the first time the children were allowed to laugh and make noise without being hushed in days. He was treated like a returning hero and he felt the part. Fortunately, d'Oria was in a tavern in town and Scacciato did not have to face him before the arrest. With his brother gone, Capece dead, and d'Oria in prison, he was the head of the family. He warmed to the position instantly, as if he had only taken a break for three days, dangling in a stone tomb.

The next morning he appeared before the council and was stunned to hear them ask to take the governorship temporarily. The council members, without a center like Capece, were apprehensive about the approach of the new king. Whether it was legal or not, they voted him acting governor and presented him with a written proclamation to that effect. Scacciato accepted it without a thought, sent them home, and with Alfonse's help began to sort through the confusion of tedious details that the governor had to consider. They worked very late and spent the night in the governor's chambers so that they could begin again in the morning. Scacciato - the Outcast - had taken power.

Midway through the second morning of work, since he did not know when the new king would arrive, Scacciato took care of an important duty. He wrote and signed an order of execution for d'Oria and, brushing aside Alfonse's timid suggestion that it might not be entirely legal, set the time for the hanging at ten the following day, so as to assure that there would be a good crowd in the square.

Later in the day, a messenger brought word that King Frederick was on the other side of the island with a small army of Spaniards but would be at least two days before reaching the capital. Scacciato did not know what the new king's intentions were or what, if any, interest he would have in the murderer of the governor he hated, but Scacciato was relieved nonetheless that d'Oria would be good and dead long before King Frederick arrived. He sent word to Emelia to stay at the mansion and that he would return to her the following evening. Not thinking, simply acting, he threw himself into the work with Alfonse. They settled minor disputes all day, answered questions from merchants and former cronies of Capece, signed various proclamations, and organized a greeting party to meet the new king outside of town. His last duty was to plan a ceremony in the square for Frederick, the man who might have him killed.

VIII

It was a beautiful day for a hanging. The sun was out but a speckled sky full of rapidly-moving pure white clouds kept the day from becoming too hot. The gusting wind added to the feeling of activity and anticipation. Long before ten, the square was bustling: merchants and farmers, the well-off and the peasants, those who had hated Capece and those who had loved him. They all mingled in the carnival of execution. Bakers sold pies, wine merchants kept the early morning crowd tipsy, and puppeteers in horse-drawn carts set up their preliminary entertainment in each corner of the square.

Through it all, the talk: did Scacciato really take the blame for d'Oria? did d'Oria really kill Capece or was it someone else? was it part of some cabal? was Scacciato's aim all along to replace his father as governor? what would the new King do? was he really a cripple as they said and was he really a secret Papist as they said and did he really keep prostitutes as they said? and where were the women, the women of the mansion, the child-bride Emelia, the deer-woman Cavriuola, the lusty widow Spina and why did none of them come to watch the destruction of the old man's murderer? will it rain today? how is your mother? how are your crops? how is your gout? will he scream and beg forgiveness? will his eyes pop out when the rope tightens around his neck?

Scacciato dressed himself lethargically in the bedchambers of the governor's office where he had slept for two nights. He was exhausted from the work and from trying not to ask himself the question that lingered in his mind: why had he done it? He had found his freedom in a prison cell, he was through with hate and revenge. Yes, he wanted to live, but at what price? Was his survival, a forgotten value only days before, of utmost importance simply because an opportunity had presented itself? And in the background, the uncertainty, the curiosity about the new king and what would happen upon his arrival, gnawed at him, flared up in his thoughts. Well, he thought as he started out the door of the bedroom, you certainly have thrown yourself back into the world in full force.

He sat down behind the governor's desk, listlessly leafing through papers, until he heard the noise and the jeering of the crowd outside. Alfonse had told him he was going to ride out early in the day, before dawn, to see if any of the governor's guard he used as scouts had any information about King Frederick's approach, but had planned to be back for the hanging. He was not.

Scacciato walked through the deserted building alone and made his way through the front door packed with idlers and beggars, then into the crowd. As he pushed his way forward, everyone saluted and cheered him, encouraged him to get right up front to watch it closely and enjoy every second of the event. He smiled and nodded as people let him pass, cleared a corridor in the mob for the new governor, the son of the man whose murder would be avenged. Even though they stepped back for him, the press of the crowd was stifling, the smell of their sweat nauseating, the sound of their cries of excitement disgusting to him. His face settled into a parody of a smile, a gritted contortion of the face which made the eyes seem darker and more recessed, his blade of a nose even larger. He acknowledged no one; it was as if he was in a sea of strangers, all screaming at him, sweating on him, breathing wine-sour breath in his face, slapping him on the back with hands like whips. In minutes he had crossed the square and stood a few feet in front of the wooden platform which was occupied by only two men. The hangman, a surprisingly frail-looking man, wore a drab green tunic. He had thinning hair and a mouth full of teeth like broken nuts. d'Oria wore a gray robe. He slouched as sloppy and fat as ever, puffy-faced, either from sleepless nights or the absence of alcohol. His hands and feet were perfunctorily bound. The thick rope - Scacciato's rope - hung around his sallow, drooping neck. Scacciato stood for only a moment before the crowd cleared in front of him and he was left with no one between him and d'Oria.

He looked up at the man, saw him focus his reddened beady eyes on his murderer. d'Oria drooled, then twitched along the side of his face.

Scacciato tried to read the expression in d'Oria's eyes, tried to fathom whether there was hatred there or whether d'Oria had gone entirely mad and did not even understand anymore what was happening. But there was no more there that made sense, that seemed human, than there ever had been. The crowd began to shout behind him: "NOW, NOW, NOW!"

From behind him, the roar felt as if it would blow him over like the gusting wind. From in front of him, the insanity of it all, the past, the slavery, the murder, the emptiness of d'Oria and Capece and their world was refracted through d'Oria's mad eyes, burning Scacciato's face like the sun. I could save this man's life with a word, he thought. But I won't.

No one understood why the young man did what he did, turned and fought his way through the crush, refused to enjoy the spectacle, although they would talk about it for years. No one knew why even when the roar of the throng must have told him that the rope was taut and d'Oria was squirming in the wind he did not look back and there was no change in his expression, that look that some described as lunacy, some as disgust, and others as simple nausea. Years later, almost everyone who had been at the hanging and some who were not claimed to have been shoved aside by Scacciato as he forced his way through the crowd, although he could not have reached them all. Some claimed to have seen him take the first horse he saw and ride away, others said they saw him running in the direction of the mansion, others said he walked aimlessly around in the back of the square where it was less crowded. No one remembered seeing him walk quickly to the alley between the prison and the building next to it, to the very alley which had been his only source of light and had constituted an element of his freedom a few days before. After he was out of sight, no one thought of Scacciato; there was death to watch and life would always be around tomorrow.

In the alley his constitution failed him and he stumbled, ran a few steps, stopped and looked ahead. He saw a large flower urn forgotten in the alley and full of tiny green weeds a few feet further on. He thought that if he could make it to that urn he could sit and feel well again. He took a step and an ocean of confusion and loathing welled up inside; he leaped forward as far as he could but as he did sharp pain sliced through his head and his stomach rose to choke off his breath. He fell to the ground on his hands and knees and vomited into the reddish dirt, saw through his tears the puddle beneath him and the speckles on his hands made by the splattering of wet dust. He heard the crowd and their wailing. He smelled their sweat as if they were still pressed against him though it was his own sweat raining on to the ground beneath him that he smelled. He saw d'Oria's swollen face every time his body wrenched, and he threw up again and again and again and again. For a few moments he could not see for the tears, he could not think for gasping, and he could not hear for the ringing in his ears like a church bell gone beserk. Then it subsided. He thought that between gasps he could feel something, sense a presence, hear something, perhaps the sound of heaving or short breathing. With all his strength, he tightened his entire body and held himself as still as a wild animal for a few seconds, trying with both his mind and his body to understand what it was.

"Hey asshole."

Time stopped. He heard a voice. It was from the past. He could not bear to look up but he knew he must. He tried to take deep breaths to prepare himself and to stop the heaving of his chest. He spat and cleared his throat, spat again and raised his head. Blurry, through wet eyes, unbelievably, there he was: Little Vision, wearing the same shabby ill-fitting clothes. He jumped up on the rim of the urn and crossed his short legs. He wiggled his fingers in a more pleasant greeting than the one he had uttered.

"You look terrible, Scacciato," he gurgled, then laughed. "It's quite a mess you've made, eh?" He laughed again.

"You." Scacciato glared through the tears.

"Are you going to kill the rest of them now or are you going to take a break?"

"I would ..." He had to spit. "I would like to kill you."

"Never learn, do you, you little bist? When do the feet come up? What about the legs and the belly? Then those hate-filled eyes, perhaps we'll finally see what's really behind them. I would love to stick around for the lips but heaven help us when that nose pops out. It could split a tree in half."

For an instant, Scacciato feared that all the Christians had been right: there was a hell and he was in it. Despite the years of work, training, scheming, risk-taking, murder, prison, and brilliant escape, he was still being insulted by an ugly dwarf.

"They made me sick," he said, not knowing why he suddenly

had to confide in Little Vision. "The mass of them, the mob of them, all crying for death, for entertainment, all cheering me on as I committed murder the second time. The smell of them, the sound of them... "

"Of course they made you sick, you little shit. What did you expect from them? Honor? Morality? Sanity? Surely you have learned something about people through all these years. No? Well, there is time. But I will grant you this. You have showed some ... what should I say? You have shown ... cleverness? No, that's not it. Perhaps ... hmmm ... no ... but perhaps ... ingenuity? Ah yes, ingenuity. Maybe guile or cunning would be a better way to put it." He paused and pondered for a moment. Scacciato loathed the fact that Little Vision still had not learned to decide on his words. "Oh never mind. The point is... well, Scacciato, I'm not sure what the point is. But I did tell you the truth all those years ago, did I not?"

"What truth?" Nothing seemed true to Scacciato at the moment.

"About yourself, you ninny. About the world, about your life, about little creatures that repeat themselves over and over. Think about it, son. Wouldn't old Capece be proud of you and all you have done?"

"You bastard." Something was descending on his back and shoulders but he did not know if it was hatred again or shame or simply the deepest feeling of confusion a man can feel.

"Names, poo." He waved his hand to make Scacciato's words go away. "But don't you know you had to make the same mistakes? You had to, you know. It's ... it's the way things are, I guess. At least it certainly seems that ... in my experience, it's always, well almost always that way. But don't you see ..." He sat up on the rim of the urn, uncrossed his legs, and wiggled them in the air. "Can't you see that the point is not whether you will make the same mistakes as your father, not whether you will become incredibly like him while you hate and deny the thought like a poison. That is not the question." He leaned his head closer to Scacciato and stared at him. After a few moments, his face lost its look of omniscience and went blank, then quizzical, as if he had forgotten what came next.

"What is the question? Finish, damn you!" Scacciato started to slam his fist into the dirt but looked down at the quagmire and thought better of it.

"Yes, of course." He sat back and thought. "You were always so impatient." His eyes became dull like those of a dying bird, then lit up again, pigeon-mad. "Yes, of course! It is not a question of whether or not you will make the same mistakes but when you will catch on. Don't you see? We all make the same mistakes as our fathers, of course we do. But some of us stop doing it sooner than others. Some, of course, like the bist, never stop. Some stop when they are your age, though most don't. Some stop when they are much older. Some only when they are very old and have to be fed by strangers. That, my little friend, is the question. When do you stop?"

"Now, damn it!" He was on his hands and knees again, oblivious to the mess in the dirt. There were tears as well but they were tears of pleading, tears begging Little Vision to let him stop. "I want to stop now!"

"There, there, my boy," he said, softly. "I know it's hard. But perhaps you have learned a lot, perhaps you do understand at last. But understand this." He had never sounded as serious before in his two visits to Scacciato. "Even after you stop making the mistakes, playing the same scenes over and over, so much has been set in motion that your life will never be entirely free of it, free of the things you have done, free of the choices and stupid wrong turns you have made. There is simply too much that you have to follow through as it is because you have already done things which cannot be undone. That does not mean you are not free to choose, free to act in response to what will happen. You are. Quite definitely. But it is simply this..."

A voice from the distance interrupted. Scacciato looked down at the ground to concentrate, to hear who it was. The crowd was quieter now, only a low hum in tha background. There was a single voice, cutting through that hum. It was Alfonse, crying out Scacciato's name. He knew he was too weak to call to him. Instead, he looked up at Little Vision. "It is simply what?"

He smiled a tiny smile. "It is not over."

"Scacciato! Scacciato!" The voice was closer; Scacciato turned his head to look at the alley threshold. In an instant, Alphonse was framed in the entrance. He stopped and glanced in Scacciato's direction. "Scacciato, my friend!" He ran toward the young man kneeling in the acrid dirt.

Scacciato felt a relief he had not known since entering the prison when he saw the massive Alphone running toward him. Then he thought: Little Vision! He can see Little Vision! He spun around and saw the urn, full of weeds, only tiny green weeds that were not crushed by the weight of anyone sitting upon them. He could not take his eyes off the urn until Alphonse, squatting beside him, shook him by the shoulder.

"Scacciato, you are sick," he said tenderly. "My poor friend, this has been too much for you. But you will probably feel better, now that you have been sick, right?"

"Yes," he said absently. "I am better now."

"Are you really all right?"

"Yes." He wiped his forehead and was surprised at how wet it was. "I am all right. Where have you been?"

"My friend, I hate to tell you this at this moment, with you just being sick and all, but there is no time to waste. You must know now. The wretched Spaniard, he is not far from here, no more than a day. And he is belching proclamations already. My guardsmen intercepted one of his messengers and before they slit the scoundrel's throat, they wrestled away his message. Frederick has ordered you dead. Actually, he ordered for both of the sons of the governor to be executed on sight, put a bounty on both your heads. The rest of the family, the women and the children, will be graciously spared, the worthless bastard says. But he ordered that both you and Giusfredi must die to rid the island of insidious influences of the past." He looked down as if he did not want to state the obvious while looking Scacciato in the eye. "He does not know about Giusfredi."

"Of course."

Alfonse did not know if the "of course" referred to the last sentence or to his entire relating of events. "What will you do? You must leave at once. You must leave the island."

Scacciato did not have to think about what he would do; he already knew. It was as if he had always known. "Yes. I know people on the coast. I have more than enough contacts and gold to get a ship on a moment's notice. I will ride to the coast tonight." He shifted his weight. "Help me, Alfonse, and ride with me to the mansion to say goodbye."

He lifted the soaked and reeking Scacciato to his feet. "Do you wish me to come with you abroad? I will serve you more faithfully than I ever served your father."

He leaned against the man's chest as a child leans against his father. "No, you wonderful creature. You have your own life. Or you can start to have it now. Disappear, blend into the crowd, they will never know you were with Capece. You do not have the stain of his blood. Find a wife, have children, raise some crops. You deserve a peaceful life."

"Yes." Alfonse understood that for the second time Scacciato had given him his freedom. "Come, I will find horses while you go inside and clean up. I will be at the back of the square waiting when you are ready."

Scacciato stood on his own at last. The two men walked down the alley without speaking. At the entrance, he stopped and looked back at the urn. He squinted his eyes, then opened them wide.

"What is it, Scacciato?"

"A vision, that's all. Just a little vision. Let us go."

* * *

He made love to Emelia once more, sadly and softly, while a servant in the next room kept Giusfredi and listened. Afterwards they dressed silently and went into the next room. Emelia took the infant from his nurse and sent her away. Scacciato held his face close to the child's as he had on the night of his birth. Always, Giusfredi loved to run his baby fingers along Scacciato's face, feeling the topography of his father, laughing as he did, gurgling the uncomplicated laugh of the infant. Scacciato lighlty nibbled on the child's nose.

"Ah Giusfredi, named for a dead man, son of an outcast, what will become of you? Perhaps you will hate me though I will try to change the world to keep it from being so. It seems that we are in a cycle, little one, you and I, but cycles are meant to be broken. I will fight to break all the cycles I can discover. Perhaps I will fail. Perhaps it will fall on you. I don't know. I cannot know, nor can you. But I will be back somehow. You have not seen the last of this monstrous face your fingers know so well."

He put his arms around Emelia and the child at the same time, squeezed them lightly, and looked at his wife. "You will be all right, Emelia. Alfonse says the proclamation spares you and the rest of the household. It is only me that the new king must kill. You know where the keys to the vault are. Use the gold wisely. Hide some away. Be careful of who you trust, even Spina and Cavriuola."

"Yes." She looked at her husband imploringly as if he could change it all, make all the trouble go away. "You are sure we should not come with you?"

"Nonsense. Here you have safety and comfort and wealth. Out there I do not know what I will face. Besides, the Spaniards will hunt me, at least for a while, and you will be safer here where they can keep an eye on you, expecting me to return. Out there we may find ourselves on some black night road with no one but a cutthroat assassin to deal with and he might not remember the details of a king's proclamation about sparing women and children. The road is no place for a woman and an infant. Stay here and think of me. Raise my son and try to explain it to him when you think he will understand."

"I will, Scacciato." They exchanged glances but both looked down quickly. "We will send old Anglico with you to the coast so he can report back to us that you have escaped."

"He may be in danger riding with me."

"No. No one knows him. If there is danger he can simply ride away and once you are gone they will see only an old gardener riding back from the coast. He will be all right. But I must know that you get away. I could not live not knowing for sure."

He nodded and stepped away from her. He started to put his arms around her again but did not. There had to be a last time. "With all my heart, I promise you will see me again, Emelia."

She could not speak or move. She could only watch him walk through the door and listen to his footsteps down the corridor. It was a sound she would think of for years, long after the embers of hope had burned out.

The women were gathered in the dusk on the back porch of the mansion. Old Anglico, wearing the work clothes he used in the garden, waited with two horses at the foot of the perron. Scacciato spoke to them first as a group.

"I want you all to help Emelia. She is young and although she is strong there is much for her to endure. She will need your help. And take care of my son, of course. Raise him to be his own man. Do not pamper him or spare him the truth. But please give him all the affection he will need. Let him know he is loved." He turned to Spina and they embraced. Her breasts pressed against him and he felt both desire and anger as he thought of how she had held both his brother and his father. But there was no use in torturing her or himself. "Goodbye, Spina. Take care of your children." She looked at him, fully aware that he knew about her affair with Capece, and did not speak.

He held his mother and felt the lightness, the fragileness of her body. When he pulled back to look in her eyes, he realized that she had been through all of this before in a different life, before she constructed the magical forest inside her mind where she lived and would live for the rest of her days.

"My son," she whispered. "I love you. Do not come back."

He stepped back and wondered. Does she know, does she truly understand what is happening? I do not know, but there will be plenty of time to think about it. He moved away from her.

The old Nurse smiled at him pleasantly when he turned to her, as if he was going off to an academy or a sporting match instead of leaving to drift across a continent with executioners on his trail. He hugged her but could not think of what to say, nor could she. They hugged again and he promised "I will send your old gardener back to you safely." She smiled, glancing down the steps at her lover.

Scacciato ran down the steps, checked to be sure that Anglico had put the right bags on the horse, and mounted. He rode away without another look or word, leaving Anglico to throw himself on his horse and gallop to catch up with him.

They were a quarter of a mile away before Scacciato reigned in his horse, turned in the saddle, and glared back at the mansion with both anguish and hope in his eyes.

Anglico grinned as if he knew what Scacciato was thinking. "There is always an easier path to follow, Scacciato. But we do not know that until we've nearly reached the end."

Scacciato nodded and touched his horse with his heels. Then they traveled on together down the road to the coast. One old, one young, one glancing back over his shoulder, one gazing toward the sea.